LYNN HESSE

D0816137

This publication is fiction. Any name associated with a real person is purely unintentional.

© 2022 Lynn Hesse All rights reserved.
LynnHesse.com

This publication may not be reproduced, stored in a retrieval system, or transmitted in whole or in part, in any form or by any means, electronic, mechanical, photocopying, recording, or otherwise, without the prior written permission of Lynn Hesse or the Publisher. Short quotations may be used by newspapers, magazines, and other publications, and online blogs as part of reviews, articles, or reports, but must attribute author and book title. For permissions, write: BlueRoomBooks@outlook.com
Subject Line: Forty Knots

Cover design and interior layout: Angela K. Durden
Editors: Tom Whitfield and Angela K. Durden

ISBN: 978-1-950729-18-0

THE FORTY KNOTS BURN
LYNN HESSE
BLUEROOMBOOKS.COM
DECATUR, GEORGIA

9 781950 729180

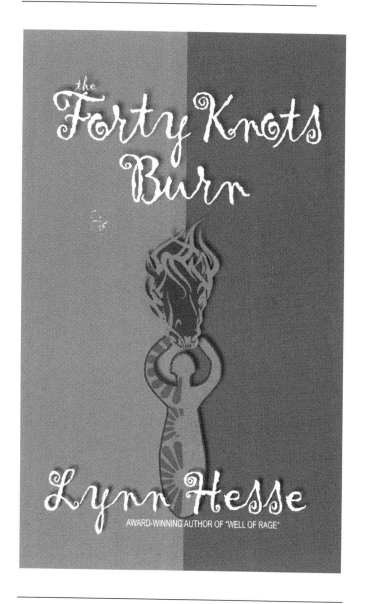

the

Forty Knots Burn

Lynn Hesse

AWARD-WINNING AUTHOR OF "WELL OF RAGE"

Glossary of Terms

Roma Terms

Ando foro: In town

Gadje: All non-Roma are referred to by the term gadje; also spelled gadze or gaje; the term is pejorative meaning bumpkin, yokel, or "barbarian".

Mochadi: Spiritually and ceremonially unclean, defiled, dirty.

Roma: Noun: a people originating in South Asia and traditionally having an itinerant way of life, living widely dispersed across Europe and North and South America and speaking a language (Romani) that is related to Hindi. "The Roma have a strong cultural heritage." Adjective: Of or relating to the Roma or their language.

Sinti: In this novel, Roma clans settled in communities are referred to as Sinti.

The Sinti (also Sinta or Sinte; masc. sing. Sinto; fem. sing. Sintesa) are a Romani people in Central Europe that number around 200,000. Traditionally itinerant, today only a small percentage of Sinti remain unsettled. In the past, they lived on the outskirts of communities, but now often live within. They were first mentioned in 1100 by an Arab historian. An ethno-linguistic group that is one of the oldest Indian Subcontinent diasporas in Europe.

Russian Terms

Blyat: The root of the word means wander around, referring to a woman who sleeps around. The original meaning refers to a woman of a certain ancient profession but is not used in that sense. It is more of an exclamation that can be used separately or as part of a sentence; akin to f*ck.

Moya lyubov: Loved one, or spare the life of my loved one.

Nyet: Russian for no. "Da nyet" is mainly used to say "no" in Russian when the speaker is undecided but seems to lean more in the direction of a negative answer.

Croatian Terms

Grappa: Made from the grape variety Moscato/Muskatela. 40% Alc. Mild in taste, fruity, very delicious. Is a 100% natural product, without any additives or coloring. It serves as the perfect finale for any meal and in Croatia they use the Moscato Grappa as a welcome drink.

Kunas: Croatian coins or money. One kuna equals 15 cents in U.S. dollars.

Rakija: Serbo-Croatian name given to an alcoholic drink made from distillation of fermented fruit. A clear-as-water drink, with a percentage of alcohol that can range from approximately 40% to 65%, a high-alcohol version of grappa.

Ando foro

I am a thief. I don't break into your house and steal your things. Much more scandalous, I'm charming and smooth. I give you the show you desire, but are too afraid to ask for. I see your most secret wish, and I use probability and fate to slip the money from your hand as I make you believe your future will be happy, contented, perhaps adventurous; a shiny, wondrous thing to behold.

I am a fortune teller extraordinaire. I know my craft, my trade. I do not feel guilty. When has your kind ever felt badly about spitting on my so-called heathen people? You call us dirty names in the light of day but sneak into our camps and businesses at night, begging for our healing potions and advice. I can't respect you. I pity the *gadje*. I save my ancient Roma curses for more worthy opponents, stronger devils than you.

Schooled by the best Roma clans in Europe in the foothills where the French and Spanish borders meet, my parents immigrated to America in 1957 with me inside my mother's belly. After nearly starving on the road, they settled in a community with their distant cousins, a non-traveling Roma sect, the Sinti in Dune Park, Indiana. It is there I, Amorosa Bauminavick, become known as the old matchmaker.

I am now *ando foro*, that is in town, to see the woman of whom I am the Great Aunt and Godmother, Miss Clara Shannesy Blythe, whose most-interesting story begins now.

Of course the locker room maid blamed me for the rash of petty thefts from the lockers. "You and your kind need to keep moving on and leave Atlanta," Miss Sadye said.

I didn't like this woman's biased attitude about me or my Roma people, but I shouldn't be surprised at it; minorities all over the world compete for their piece of the pie and look down on others like the privileged few do to all of them. After all, I had done the same: Spitting into the clan gathering's fire as a child I had called a Jewish man *kike* after he refused to pay my mother's price for a potion.

Standing toe to toe, I scanned up Sadye's chest. Craning my neck to see her face, I felt the blood and shame rush to my own. "Go bother someone who cares what you think," I said, but my accuser never looked at me.

She yelled "Maintenance" and sent the old patrons into a slow-moving panic. They wrapped towels and stuffed drooping boobs into whatever was handy. One of the senior twins, both doubles for Marlene Dietrich, stepped on her sister's bunion. Her sister screamed and cursed, pulling up her skirted swimsuit, and slammed the locker shut so hard the woman next to them called security on her cell. Even last week at the pool, the old scrawny guy wearing a red Speedo doing laps didn't cause the brouhaha Hernando Alves generated as he entered the Ladies locker room to unplug a toilet.

I felt a smidgeon of compassion for the khaki-clad Hispanic custodian. His premature salt-and-pepper hair and broad shoulders caused fluttering in my pelvic regions and consumed most of my attention. I wanted the man to look up at my slim figure in my new bathing suit. I'd bought the chic black and white number a few months ago on my twenty-seventh birthday in Dallas and wanted his dark eyes to slide all over me.

But he kept his eyes riveted on his boots while he followed the yellow-brick center tiles through the domain of startled women suited up in spandex and flowered shower caps, ready for their arthritis exercises. Music coming from overhead speakers started playing the hymn *Sinnerman*; the song mixed with the hum of onlookers straining and stretching to see into the stall. The noise hit a crescendo as I nudged sideways to an open vantage point in the swarm and spied his flexing bicep. He punched the plunger down into the bowl for the last time. Swoosh. A successful flush.

Desire built somewhere near my abdomen and the absurdity of it hit me in the same moment. I swallowed. It must be my biological clock ticking and male pheromones in the air. I needed to get ahold of myself and remain low key until the boss felt better and he decided when we should leave Atlanta. The three Golden Rules couldn't be broken: No cons without Victor. No pulling up stakes without running money. And no dating without a background check. The principles even seemed sound in my enraptured state.

Sadye, a headstrong force, could have been in her fifties or sixties. With a shedding mop in her hand, she pushed her way through the throng of thick bodies. "Get in the pool or wrap a towel around yourself for heaven sakes," she said to me and then zeroed in on Hernando. The throng of women standing nearby stopped to watch the show and were drawn into the drama. They followed the self-appointed moral guidance counselor, with me trailing behind.

She shook the gray strings of the mophead over the male interloper. "You better get on, now." He dodged the mop when Sadye turned about face with her weapon of choice over her shoulder like a cadet in drill formation. "Ain't nothing here for you to see," she said so close I could've counted the hairs on her chin.

As the custodian ducked his head into his forearms and tried to thread his way through the crowd, he brushed Sadye's chest. "Men are just lustful dogs," she said and hit Hernando about his back and shoulders with the dirty strings.

My evil twin took over my body. Possessed as if this man was my lover, I stepped behind Sadye and struck the back of her knee with one of mine causing her to collapse on top of Hernando. The heap of long arms and beanpole legs in the floor didn't move for three heartbeats. The clump of women became a shrill staccato siren.

I held Sadye's waist and lifted one of her arms around my shoulders as Hernando looped the limp woman's other arm around his neck. He apologized over and over for any inconvenience he might've caused, as we gingerly sat Sadye on a bench.

"Get back. Give her some room," I said to the clucking onlookers.

"I'm all right. I don't think I broke anything," Sadye said, straightening her smock over her ample breasts, "but Clara, you better cover up and go fetch someone from the front desk. They'll want a report."

"Right." I dusted myself off.

She patted Hernando's bicep and shot me a sly smile. "Mr. Alves will stay right here with me."

As I left to do her bidding I whispered a curse I thought I'd long forgot, "May your valuables become worthless or unusable."

I tried not to squirm on the MARTA bus while I sat next to a fortyish-looking nun in an updated half-habit getup and worn orthopedic tie shoes. The nun caught my eye and nodded her approval toward *The Screwtape Letters* hardback lying in my lap. I smiled underneath a yawn and turned my attention away but caught a whiff of faux optimism and incense. The tic of flicking her thumb and forefinger indicated to me she was on meds. I fantasized at some point she was a divorcee, and her house in the burbs felt empty. Being an empty nester or childless and probably without marketable skills, she decided to devote herself to God's work. I envisioned her praying for her ex, perhaps, an incompetent junior devil like Wormwood. Victor, my mentor, knew I was good at reading people, not unlike Screwtape in that regard. That's why he trained me to be a psychic reader.

My mother and great aunt hadn't passed on how to use my family's psychic gift of sight before I ran away at fourteen, but the actual knowledge I lacked I compensated for by using my mentor's theatrical techniques. In his day, before a drunken brawl between a powerful director and Victor, he had been a respected British Shakespearean actor. I suspected they were lovers, and the man ruined Victor's career over a silly misunderstanding.

"If you know a man's desire, you know his weakness." My Roma pop had a fondness for the saying. As an exercise, I wondered about each person as they got on the bus and paired the best con in my repertoire with the right mark.

A free palm reading in the field, mentioning a curse was seen within the lines of the client's hand, got their attention. "It was hanging over their heads" I'd say and then suggest money be brought in a small paper bag for the ritual necessary to lift the curse. Usually it worked. Switching out the bag full of cash with a sleight of hand and replacing it with another bag full of paper was easy enough because of the mark's fear, a sure-fire motivator that made them distractable.

Women getting on the bus with multiple packages that left their tote bags wide open and their wallets within reach distracted me. I resisted the temptation to practice my pickpocketing skills and, instead, swapped C. S. Lewis' tale for my journal. I put my backpack between me and the nun, wrote so tiny the nun couldn't decipher my manuscript. She kept peering over, trying to get a glimpse, but I used my shoulder to block her sight.

I thought about my favorite marks for my sleight-of-hand or shell game as the bus passed by strip shopping malls and condo construction sites. Occasionally, I picked a pocket or lifted a Rolex or gold chain from despicable pimps or drug dealers in bus or train stations. Like my adopted uncle Roman would say in Russian when describing bad men in power, "He who feeds the pig also holds the knife over it when it is fattened."

I wrote in my journal:

> Once in New Orleans I took a Beretta 9mm from the back waistband of a foul-mouthed pimp trying to seduce a young runaway into what he called the "good life" but was in truth underage prostitution. The lowlife scum was bent forward with his elbows on his knees. As he inched forward, the Latino girl, maybe fifteen, sitting on the opposite bench drew back further and further until her dark hair seemed to fade into the wood grain. After I lifted the gun, I acted like I was the girl's aunt arriving a bit late, then I bought the girl a triangular-

shaped sandwich from the vending machine. When I handed her some money rolled around a card with a runaway helpline number, I added some advice, my mistake. I danced around domestic violence and incest issues, adhering to the taboos in my Roma upbringing. Naming such things gave power to them. I suggested if there had been any mistreatment at home the teenager would be safe because the staff counselor would place her in foster care, not send her back to her family.

She got a cynical look on her cherub face. "You mean sexual abuse," she said, mocking me. "So you think the system protects kids like me? Just ditched a pair of foster perverts in an upscale neighborhood off Hickory Street." The girl shook her head and left without another word.

I had felt crummy as she walked away. The girl looked disheveled, like she slept too many nights on the streets, missing shelter cutoff times and remaining nameless like the many who were left standing in line as the shelter reached its maximum bed-to-people ratio.

I closed my journal and, as any good con artist would, paid attention to my environment. Now, stranded in Atlanta for the last few months because of Victor's health problems, I knew this city was a hub for sex trafficking. *I wondered how Miss Latino was, wherever she was, or if she was still alive?* A person can make it by eating one meal a day, but the streets take away your pride and rob you of hope. I know. I must have looked desperate thirteen years ago to Victor and Roman, the day we met on the Dune Park Express Train headed for Chicago.

When the bus stopped at Covington Highway and Panola Road, I got off. My hotel was near Panola and I-20, half a mile away, but I needed some alone time. A walk would do me good before I met up with Roman at the hotel diner. I worried about Victor. I couldn't visualize my world functioning without either Victor the Great or Uncle Roman, our road manager and chief cook and bottle washer. I wanted everything to remain the same. Victor had to survive the surgery and recover his steady step and grand manner.

Two days later a floor nurse at DeKalb General Hospital told me Victor was sleeping and not to disturb him. I wanted to be in his hospital room when he woke up. Walking down the hall, I took shallow breaths, inhaling as little as possible of the bland sanitized world inside the medical facility. The distracted expression on the face of the doctor who passed by and the institutionalized tile-floored hallway blurred. My vision narrowed and grew foggy. I stopped and leaned against a disgustingly green wall. Swallowing hard, I breathed through my mouth to control my urge to puke.

I hoped Roman would be inside the hospital room, tucked in a chair, working crossword puzzles, watching over Victor, and waiting for me with his generous easygoing manner.

I shuffled a plant and *The New Yorker* in my hands, and managed to push open the door losing only a few bits of dirt from the flowerpot. Roman stared at me, but only for a moment. It dawned on me how ridiculous I appeared. Yes, Victor loved orchids and had even purchased an annual pass to the Atlanta Botanical Garden. Something we travelers never do, because planning that far in advance is a commitment we won't honor. Here I came carrying a potted orchid, in the Australian Dendrobium family, one more item to drag and care for on the road or leave behind.

"You look pale. You okay, Tinkerbelle?" Roman asked.

I nodded. Without showing a hint of judgment, Roman took the orchid in his huge, thick-fingered hands and arranged the pot on the window ledge. He offered to buy me coffee and a Danish from the cafeteria and disappeared. His discretion allowed me to recover from the overwhelming emotions I felt gazing at Victor's pallid, slumbering countenance. The surgeon told us Victor's heart attack had damaged over half his heart. Anger washed over me. A perceptive man like Victor must have dismissed the early warning signs until it was too late. It would explain his strange decision to stay in Atlanta "for a bit longer" and enjoy the Cherry Blossom Festival in Macon. I was digging in my purse for a tissue when Victor said, "Clara, my dear girl, you always were a noisy little beast. Come here and give me a hug."

The good news was that Victor would be expected to walk tomorrow — chest staples and all, and, if all his lab work looked good, he could leave the following day. Then Victor ushered me out with a stubborn wave of his hand. "Go keep Roman company."

I stopped at the saltwater aquarium fish tank next to the gift shop in the hospital atrium and admired the array of colors and types of the water inhabitants. Exotic fish was one of Victor's passions. Being a gig-here-and-there actor, Victor usually kept two or three fish in a mini tank in whatever hotel room we happened to be staying at. We left them when we moved on. He loved to design new underwater landscapes and to watch the fish swim. For our current room he had purchased a Blonde Naso Tang, an aggressive fellow partial to eating other fish similar in form or coloring. I named the fish Hitchcock because of its deceptive mild coloring, bulbous body, and short snout. By browsing with Victor on multiple occasions in a local pet store during the last couple of months, I had noticed he enjoyed a symbiotic pair, a pistol shrimp and a yellow, pearly jawfish. The latter species, known for swimming close to the bottom and warning blind pistol shrimp of predators, fascinated Victor. The contrast of this pair's yin versus the yang of the duplicitous Tang was the perfect idea for Victor's welcome-home gift.

Sighing, I followed an iridescent green fish with my forefinger and caught my dull reflection in the glass. I needed to get my blood pumping. Our last con was months ago in Dallas. I wondered if Roman would be amenable to a little outing, a stakeout of sorts. I hurried toward the cafeteria.

Following the judgmental locker queen for a while after work sounded like a fun idea. Because of information afforded by Sadye Mitchell's nametag and the whiteboard in the office — the preoccupied director had left the door open the last time I worked out — I knew Sadye's workday ended in about an hour, barely enough time to drive our rental car across town and wait. Roman wouldn't want to leave Victor, but I would tell him a half-truth, that I was smitten and was vetting a man as a possible suitor. Relaying the details to Roman in a way that suggested the spry Sadye might be Hernando's mother and not insult my adopted uncle's common sense would be a challenge, but he would say nothing. He loved me, and we, the tribe of only three, rarely made friends or paramours on our layovers.

I hadn't had a real lover in several years because the background checks were a headache, but I indulged in anonymous one-night stands with Roman as my bodyguard waiting in the wings in case anything went sour. According to Roman, as is the Roma custom, everyone, especially women, should be married. The fact that none of us pretended to be celibate or have any interest in marriage didn't seem to sway his opinion.

Roman sat with his back to the entrance in the cafeteria, eating a double portion of chili and beans heaped over spaghetti. After I sat down he studied my body language. He saw that I caught on to what he was doing, stood, and grabbed an extra napkin from a nearby counter.

When he returned, I said, "I'm fine, Roman. Really, I am. Victor will be better soon, and we can move on."

"Okay, but you seem antsy pants." He shrugged his wide Russian shoulders. "Nervous. Five months is long time. The longest we ever stay in one place since—"

"London, when Victor's mother died. You are perceptive. This time it's another delicate matter making me restless. There's a guy from the center where I swim. I need…I mean I want to check him out." I intentionally looked down at the table and hesitated before I continued. "He works at the gym."

"What does he do, this Romeo?"

"That's it. He doesn't know I like him. He and his mom work in housekeeping or maybe maintenance at the gym." I realized how easily I'd lied and tied Hernando to Sadye to eliminate the necessity of explaining why I yearned to pay back this horrible woman for insulting me and hitting Hernando. I babbled on. "I've even got her phone number from the community board where she posted a housekeeper-available ad with her photo."

"Victor won't like this man for you. Not a good idea."

"I am a big girl. Besides, we won't be here much longer." I locked gazes with Roman. "He seems like a nice guy. Very polite and kind of shy. Do you realize how long it has been since I went on a date? Uncle Rom, I could do it myself, but—"

"Jobs require two of us. We agreed is safer." He placed both hands on the edge of the table and squinted before he picked up his fork and waved it around. "You are twenty-seven?"

He knew my age, but I went along with the game and nodded.

"For many years I watch you. No romance. Not healthy. You need to settle down, but not with this *gadje*. Rom with Rom and *gadje* with *gadje*."

I tried to object about using a slang term for non-Roma people, but my uncle held up a palm, stopping me. He took another bite of food, chewed, and swallowed before he answered. "Okay, I agree. But only while Victor's sick. Won't hurt anyone to watch this nice guy and his family to gain their favor. Outsiders have their uses for Romas." He rubbed his fingertips together, indicating outsiders had cash, and then added, "So you talk to boss and tell him about your…janitor."

"You got it." I leaned across the table and touched his hairy forearm. "You're the best. Better than best."

"You still my Tinkerbelle?"

Grinning at him and feeling like the flighty, shrieking adolescent I was when Roman first met me, and later took me to see the Disney movie *Peter Pan*, I said, "You bet." He'd coined my pet name after commenting on how short I was and my inability to sit still, and then compared me to Disney's flying fairy, Tinkerbelle or Tink.

He patted my hand and pushed his plate away. "When do we start this checking out guy?"

"We should've left already. Remind me to undo a curse just in case it took."

Roman shook a finger at me. "Bad girl."

"Come on," I said. "His mother's shift ends at five o'clock."

2

Roman and I were in position, keeping watch. He stood beside the main entrance of the gym, smoking a cigarette while I remained in the car. I wore a pair of Jackie Onassis style glasses and a dollar store hat and tunic that made me look frumpy. Unlike European attitudes toward women, the most invisible people in America resembled women over fifty. Right now I envied them because I didn't want to be noticed.

When the automatic glass doors opened and Sadye appeared, she was talking with Hernando. I couldn't believe my luck. I opened the passenger window and flashed the lights to signal Roman. As they walked past me, I gathered through their pantomime and my eavesdropping that Hernando was escorting the old biddy home. She plopped herself in a beat-up cherry-colored Chevette that backfired as she drove off waving to Hernando, who followed in his truck. For a moment Shakespeare's green-eyed monster kicked in, but it was ridiculous to think there was any intimacy between them. He was maybe forty and movie-star handsome. Sadye was old enough to be his older sister or maybe his mother. By the time Roman dove into the driver's seat and fastened his seatbelt, I had regained my common sense and managed to say, "I think Hernando is going to fix something at her house."

He cut his eyes at me. "His mother?"

"Yes," I said, looking away. "What were the chances we could follow both of them at the same time?" As silence settled in the car, I began to question why I loathed Sadye so much. She accused me of stealing, but...I don't deny my Roma heritage. Not totally. I felt the old resentment rise within me about how my people had been treated through the ages by their so-called betters. I hated being stereotyped as an uneducated gypsy thief, a dirty outcast.

I knew Sadye looked down on me. Last month I was performing a complimentary palm reading for a prospective client in a café next to the gym when I saw Sadye pick up a to-go order. She glared her disapproval as she passed by the table. Of course, I released the client's hand and declared the game a hoot. A week later Sadye searched my bag for a swimmer's lost wristwatch.

I looked at Roman driving at the speed limit, always helpful and with my best interests in his heart. Why had I lied about Sadye to Roman? I felt mean-spirited. I said The Lord's Prayer and ad-libbed the gypsy incantation about releasing the negative energy around Sadye's assets and treasures. I had no business placing spells when I really didn't know how to undo them.

When Roman stopped and shut off the engine, I gave in to my nagging conscience and confessed I hadn't been totally transparent with him about Sadye. He grunted. "Big surprise. We talk later." Roman wasn't a fan of drama.

I focused on the surveillance.

The house was a small, rectangular shotgun house, meaning the front and back doors aligned and if the doors were open, a gunshot could theoretically pass unobstructed in a straight line through the entryway, hallway, and kitchen and exit through the back door without hitting anything. Roman, ever the astute road manager, made it his business to know his surroundings historically and geographically, and this neighborhood near Grant Park, Cabbagetown, was known for these particular types of houses.

Roman finished his short lecture. "A living room, bedrooms, and bathroom go from the hallway. Built in 1880s for Appalachian miners working in mills." My uncle barely adjusted his new binoculars before I saw Hernando appear, retrieve some tools from the pickup, and start repairing a broken step on the stoop.

Twenty minutes into his work on the warm spring evening, he stopped and stripped down to his T-shirt. My stomach felt queasy as my heartbeats fell into cadence with the working rhythm of his muscular arms and torso. Too soon he hammered the last nail into place then disappeared inside.

An hour later he left holding a pie. No doubt in lieu of payment Sadye had fed her worker dinner and had given him the pie. I held my breath as he drove away. Electricity fluttered through me. I was about to find out where my fantasy Romeo lived.

Roman glanced at me. Nothing passed by my uncle unnoticed. He kept his own counsel unless he was asked and generally said little. In this case, I was grateful. He let me savor my daydreams until Hernando parked in the driveway of a faded Victorian relic in Reynoldstown. The three-story house with a turret and egg-and-dart molding had shades of pink, purple, and green showing through the flaking outer yellow paint. Roman drove down the street, doubled back, and then slowed to a stop. There were piles of lumber and bricks stacked in the yard partially covered with tarps. "'Only in village without dogs can man walk without stick,'" Roman quoted, breaking my reverie and nodding toward the unsecured lumber.

"Probably too trusting, but I wouldn't know." I bit at a rough cuticle and forced myself to quit. "Am I acting like a silly schoolgirl?"

Roman pulled over to the curb. "No. You like him." He reached over and gently rubbed my cheek with the back of his hand. It tickled like fine sandpaper. "You want to find good spot to watch the house, or go back to hotel?"

I wanted to stay put, but Roman needed a good night's sleep. Last night he had been attending Victor and had slept in a vinyl lounge chair. Besides, an elderly neighbor opened her front door, walked down her front steps heading toward the street, and lasered in on our rental. "No," I said. "I'm hungry and both of us need some rest. We need to get an early start tomorrow to go to the hospital to see Victor. Let's call it a night." As we drove away, I noticed Hernando silhouetted in the living room window talking on the phone. So handsome.

The phone rang and rang, but I couldn't fight my way out of the floating mist of sleep. I heard our tribe's signature knock and a key unlock the door. The sun burst into the room, forcing me to cover my eyes. The smell of Roman's drugstore aftershave filled the room. He grumbled as he deposited bags of food on the kitchenette table, and the ringing ceased.

"Hello, yes," Roman barked into the phone. "Clara, get up. I am not answering service." He paused. "For you. Phone on bed." When I didn't move, he said, "I put glass of water on you. Quick. I'm busy man." He pulled the covers off me and pitched a button-down shirt at me, hitting my oversized T-shirt dead center.

"Okay, I hear you," I said, leaning across the bed and fumbling for the phone.

My Aunt Amorosa's voice jarred me wide awake. "My dear Clara, at last I have found you." I'd been safe from the family's clutches for over ten years, except when we stayed too long in one place or a letter reached me by way of a Roma friend living in North Augusta, South Carolina. I kept a P.O. box there for emergencies of a sort and my mother's rare letters. She was ashamed of her third-grade writing skills, but we kept in touch through these arduous letters transcribed by Aunt Amorosa and my infrequent phone calls to her.

Amorosa, a bloodhound, never quit sniffing out my whereabouts. Roman always registered us under aliases for that and many other reasons related to our line of work. How Aunt Amorosa knew any of our temporary addresses mystified me.

I started to drop the receiver back in the cradle, but she stopped me. "Your mother is ill. She needs you to come home. Don't hang up."

Although my aunt does have the eerie gift of telepathic vision, I thought this time she had made a lucky guess based on my past behavior of abruptly ending phone conversations with her.

"What's wrong?" I demanded. I didn't trust this woman. My mind raced, imagining the worst scenarios for my mother as my heart pounded in my chest. "Put my mother on the phone, right now, Aunt Amorosa."

"Do not speak to me as if I were a child. Your mother is dying and asks for her only daughter to be by her bedside. I delivered her message. You choose what you can live with."

The dial tone echoed in my ear.

★ ★ ★ ★ ★

Roman washed his hands, and then served me turkey sausage and eggs in our room. Under his philosophy, food made everything better and problems shrank. I declined the plate of hashbrown potatoes. "Roman, let's go to the hospital and not mention the call from Aunt Amorosa. I don't want Victor to know."

"I agree. He needs to heal. No stress. You're still worried she schemes to make you marry and have little gypsy babies?" he said with a gleam in his eye.

I flinched. The birth of a baby was the ultimate defilement and required a tent outside the living quarters or in modern times a hospital for the actual birthing process. The traveler's tent and birthing accessories were then burned. "No," I said, "her choice for me would've been to be married with half-grown children by now, but you can bet she wants something from me to ingratiate herself to the Roma king."

"Your king's name? I forget."

"Emmanuel. When I was a child, I saw him whiplash a young man for nibbling on a carrot before he washed his hands."

"You wash your hands many times in one day," Roman said.

Being an American-born Roma, or as some prefer, Sinti, I knew the clan's view, as Roman knew from his Roma Russian roots, that we weren't supposed to mingle with outsiders because they didn't follow our *marime,* laws of conduct. We followed the rules based on the beliefs our upper bodies were pure and below the waist our lower bodies were unclean, but one of my obsessions:

Hands, for obvious reasons, must be washed before touching food.

"You shouldn't be surprised about my superstitious holdovers. On both sides of my family trees can be found the European travelers," I said. "Did you know my name, Clara Shannesy Blythe, comes from my Scottish paternal ancestry?"

"Yes."

"Somewhere I have a photo of my second great-grandfather, Charles Faa Blythe, King of the Yetholm Gypsies. It's dated eighteen ninety-eight." I rummaged through my trunk. "His lineage mixed with my Hungarian grandmother's bloodline gave me jet-black hair and dark eyes." I dug out the photo. "See how tiny he looks? I guess I owe my petite size to the Scottish clan, too."

Roman touched my shoulder. "Yes, beautiful Tink," he said. "You never show me King before."

"Enough of the past." I scraped the uneaten food from my plate into the trash. "I will make the decision about whether to go home later," I said. "Amorosa is probably lying, and Mom is fine, but I need to find out for sure. Do you have any contacts who could discreetly check for me?"

"Sure. It will cost a few dollars." I understood he meant I would be expected to pay for the information with my earnings, instead of taking the fee from the general operational fund.

"No problem. I have a few hundred set aside. Can they do it within twenty-four hours?"

"I make phone call, and we see. I would do the job myself, freebie, but Victor —"

"I know. Victor and I count on you for everything. We couldn't make it without you."

He grinned. "Damn right," he said, slapping the table. "Now, get dressed. If you're not ready in fifteen minutes, I leave you."

While Roman parked the car in the hospital parking lot I noticed the pollen was thick on the cars. Someone had written WASH ME on the back windshield of a Subaru and signed the message with NEIGHBOR. Subtle. I hoped I never cared what the neighbors thought. Victor disliked the suburban lifestyle. He often said neighbors were a nuisance he couldn't abide, but those same mundane people sponsored the arts and were worthy of cultivation.

Walking down the hallway of the hospital cardiac wing with nurses pushing computers atop rolling desks, I gazed over at Roman and felt dread. Hospitals gave me the willies. Although I knew the equipment was sterilized, and the food was prepared in kitchens meeting strict health standards, visiting the sick there made me feel *mochadi* — spiritually and ceremonially unclean, defiled...dirty.

Roman jingling a few coins in his pocket caused me to wonder how low the expense kitty had gotten. Should I be scouting for a patron or mark instead of wasting time on personal matters?

Regular non-Roma folk, like the woman clutching her purse and her husband's arm walking on the far side of the hall from me, would make a good mark. Victor, a non-Roma, was the exception to this rule. An actor was as close to a gypsy as one can get without the lineage. With his theatrical training at my disposal, I'd played many parts.

Of course, Victor didn't believe in health insurance; just another government-sponsored scam. Since my eighteenth birthday, I had helped execute each scam and had benefited from an equal share; however, Roman and Victor hadn't yet discussed the family finances with me. They considered me a daughter or niece, of sorts, a person to be sheltered, not burdened with everyday details, but I knew we'd need a score soon.

Roman held the door open for me as we entered my mentor's hospital room.

Sitting in a chair, concentrating on *The New York Times* crossword puzzle, he didn't look up for a couple of seconds, but when he did he flashed his award-winning smile and smoothed the front of his silk bathrobe. "My dear ones, come give me hugs." He kissed the air near our cheeks when we bent forward to hug him. "I feel renewed. I have already walked down the hallway, to and fro, and the nurse bathed me. How do I look?"

After we profusely complimented Victor, I ventured a question. "What did the surgeon say?"

"He hasn't checked in on me today, but since I am one of his favorite patients...Yesterday, I entertained him with the story about the Paris follies; he will be by soon for another tale of passion and intrigue."

I tried to hide my irritation, but wanted an update. "So, what did he say yesterday?"

"All is well. The heart mends, as all things do, with time. My ticker is no exception. The doctor referred to a similar man who had my physical strength and dexterity living to be a hundred."

When I didn't comment, he asked me for a glass of water to break my steady gaze.

Roman clapped his bear-sized hands together and produced a map of Canada. "Clara, please clean table."

He waited for me to rub down the food tray table with a sanitized wipe I took out of my purse. Roman was a Russian Roma who didn't use a surface reserved for food for anything else, unless unusual circumstances dictated otherwise.

He flapped the map at the rolling tray until it was dry and then folded the map in half and laid it on the tray. "Boss, if you want to go to Calgary for our next stop, I get passports and place to stay like that." Roman snapped his fingers. "Nice digs. My cousin Nikkoli runs big hotsy-totsy ski resort."

As I handed Victor his glass of water, he winked at me and turned toward Roman.

"Excellent, my good man, I think the snow might be a clarifying agent after the sweet dew of Southern hospitality in Atlanta, but first we need to finish the job at hand." He held up a finger to silence us.

"Don't worry. I have every minute detail etched in my head. Absolutely marvelous how the anesthesia stimulated my brain and heightened my perceptions." He placed his fingers in a steeple formation and flexed his hands. "It's a small but lucrative project that doesn't involve me in the day-to-day operations. In fact, I spoke with Arthur yesterday, and I think you and Roman can handle the gig without me."

"A project with your brother without you?" I asked. "We've never worked with Arthur because you don't trust him."

"I don't like how Arthur talks to you," Roman said.

Victor silenced us with a wave of his hand. "Nonsense. Now, let me tell you the funny thing I overheard one of the nurses say in the recovery room."

* * * * *

The story he recounted about the recovery nurse who lost her wedding band during a tryst with a handsome patient and the ensuing fiasco of buying a substitute ring was the last thing I remember Victor saying. He died that evening, only a few hours after Roman and I left.

We were in shock after the hospital called. Roman didn't want the *gadje* to handle Victor's body any more than necessary, and neither one of us wanted an autopsy — the taking out of organs is strictly forbidden, another Roma taboo. When we arrived at the hospital, the attendant told us Victor had used his walker after dinner to traverse the hall to the nurses' station, chatting with the staff and making them laugh. An hour later a nurse found my mentor dead on the floor beside his bed.

I couldn't cry. The world felt like a blur in slow motion, but around midnight we randomly selected a funeral transport service for our dear friend's body to be removed for cremation. His previously stated choice. We asked a nurse to call Victor's brother in

New York. It was a lousy way to handle notifying Arthur, but Victor would've understood. His twin brother was an art dealer who dabbled in the black market. The man called when he needed a favor and otherwise treated Victor like the withered appendage he hid.

The next morning, I felt as hollow as Victor's cane. Roman stared at me as I shook it. Nothing slid out but a note relaying the instruction to sell his stamp collection. I put the paper in my pocket, and we left without a discussion. Roman was almost comatose and asked me to drive. On the drive to the funeral parlor to make arrangements, we decided to pawn some of our jewelry. The act of selling our valuables to pay for Victor's cremation seemed comforting, like a familiar religious rite. The bell rang when we entered and when we left. The pawnshop dealer, who knew us from other visits, seemed to sense the solemn occasion, so he didn't haggle and gave us what we asked for.

Minutes later as I gave the funeral director the cash for the fake golden crematorium urn, I realized the irony of exchanging one vessel and its contents for another. On the road — at Victor's insistence —

we carried our money and jewelry stash in a burgundy urn filled with sand that was topped off with a few leftover ashes taken from a barbeque grill. Ingenious. Nobody including traffic cops wanted to look inside or disturb the ashes.

Roman and I had agreed with Victor about using the urn trick to transport valuables, but we had argued when he had talked about a Will and had asked to be cremated. Our family clans understood the purification ritual of the burning of a body and usually added the deceased's possessions to the fire, but this was Victor, our resilient leader.

When the director asked if we wanted to see our loved one for the last time, I declined. Roman stood up, his broad shoulders held erect, and followed the squatty bald man down the long dark hallway.

Two days later, I sat holding Victor's ashes in an urn in my lap as Roman drove us back to the hotel. "All neat and tidy, this dying business," I said. "It's only been four days. Our people got this part right. At least seven days of semi-seclusion. How are we expected to move on with our lives just like that?" I turned my head and wiped a tear from my cheek.

"To hell with others," Roman said as he pushed an unruly thatched lock of hair away from his bearded face. He hadn't shaved since Victor's death, honoring the Roma custom. "I need drink," he said.

"There's vodka in the room left from Victor's birthday party but probably not enough. When is Arthur arriving?" I asked, trying not to show I was worried.

"He's flying in private plane today or tomorrow. I don't know why. He treated Victor like dog with fleas." He shrugged. "Maybe he thinks box with gold bullion waits for him."

"Fat chance. And no way I'm giving him Victor's ashes."

"Damn straight. We are family." Roman slapped his chest over his heart and reached across the center console for my hand. "Don't worry. I deal with Victor's no-good brother."

4

Drinking an espresso, Felipe Ménages sat at a local diner near the Fox Theatre in downtown Atlanta, looking out the window, waiting for his brother to arrive. Peachtree Street traffic crossed Ponce de Leon Avenue, and the urban dwellers rushed to the next appointment. A wretched homeless guy stared into the window for a moment before scratching his crotch and walking on.

A disgusting use of oxygen.

He looked at his watch and thought about Hernando's blasé attitude about time. They were nothing alike. He would do anything necessary to protect his artistic elder brother, but in his brother's presence, Felipe's competitive nature flared. Their mother favored Hernando because his father's death left the young mother heartbroken. When she married Edwin Ménages, Felipe's father, it was for security instead of love. Felipe knew his well–

traveled parents, then in their mid-forties, hadn't planned on another child. He was the surprise baby, the one that ruined all their fun.

As the remains of the espresso grew cold, Felipe committed himself to avoid his usual pattern of verbal sparring with his brother. He would offer Hernando a lucrative, under-the-table job without insisting. Funding the future of Hernando's daughter, Alexandria, and her exquisite voice, were important to both men. It was Hernando's choice to mainly support his ten-year-old daughter's dreams of being an opera singer with janitorial pay and odd jobs when his genius lay in art forgery. Felipe, as the child's godfather, could only pass along opportunities for Hernando to use his artistic skills and give financial gifts to Alexandria when allowed.

The waitress approached as Felipe's brother sat down. Batting her fake eyelashes, the redhead took Hernando's order and forgot to ask Felipe what he wanted. He felt the anger rise from his chest to his face as he commandeered the waitress. "Are you blind? Am I not sitting here?" He swept his hand in the air toward her nametag. "Pamela."

"Sorry, sir. I thought you only wanted an espresso." She clasped her hands behind her back.

"It is not for you to decide what I want or don't want. It's your job to ask."

"Please, Felipe, let this go. Just order," Hernando said as he touched his brother's elbow.

Felipe moved Hernando's arm out of the way but held his cold stare on the waitress. Glaring at Felipe, she straightened her shoulders, centering her black tie over her starched white shirt. "Of course, I apologize for my lack of attention. What would you like to order?"

After the waitress left, Hernando asked, "Have you forgotten where our parents came from? Why must you bully people? You have everything at your disposal, traveling the world with your import-export business, not to mention your other shadier endeavors. That young woman meant no harm." Hernando paused as he unfolded his cloth napkin and placed it in his lap. "I love you, but you make yourself smaller by belittling others who work with their hands."

Felipe raised his cupped hands, kissing the air as if bestowing a blessing on Hernando. "If you will listen to my low-risk proposal all the way until the end for Alexandria's sake, I will beg Pamela's forgiveness and give her a big tip."

Hernando crossed his arms. "I should've known," he said. "I will try to keep an open mind."

Victor died in late March and left us behind. The world felt askew, cocked to one side, as if I would fall off the planet at any minute. Roman acted as if he couldn't move about in his usual patterns and refrained from cooking. Takeout became the norm.

Weeks passed as Roman and I drank vodka, ate fast food, and viewed a lot of movies in a variety of cheap motels in and around Atlanta. Why Arthur didn't show up, neither of us cared enough to comment. Swimming at the gym and my interest in Hernando seemed a lifetime ago. One day in the middle of April, Roman woke me up from a nap in a dumpy motel room on Candler Road near I-20 to tell me he only had twenty dollars in cash left, and the rent was due for the week. When I tried to roll over and go back to sleep, he began to make grunting noises as he tossed the beer cans and liquor bottles outside. When the first wave of bottles hit the pavement, producing a deafening racket and creating a broken glass collage between the parked cars, Roman yelled, "Enough. Pity party is over."

He threw anything within his reach into the parking lot, including my clothes. I grabbed our toaster from his hands. He stopped. Our eyes met.

He said, "Outside. We breathe the air today."

As it turned out, we didn't have a choice. The co-managers, the Patel brothers, appeared in our open doorway and demanded we vacate the premises.

An hour later, over coffee and toast in a nearby restaurant, we discussed our options. Moving to another city with an empty bankroll ignored one of Victor's staunchest operating rules. We could run a quick bait and switch scam and risk being nailed by the cops, or, as much as we hated the idea, contact Arthur and see if the job Victor had mentioned was still available, but that would require a stake. Roman's fake green card had expired, leaving me as the only candidate to get a real job for a few weeks through a temp service, a last resort. My drinking partner at some point during our binge had already disabled the rental car's tracking device, but the service would report the car stolen soon unless we paid the bill. In the end, we decided against pawning the rest of our personal jewelry in lieu of selling some of Victor's stamp collection. We already knew an honest dealer who wanted to add it to his collection.

As we rode to the dealer's Buckhead store with Victor's prized possession, I felt the incongruence of regret and relief. My conscience in high gear reminded me I hadn't checked on my supposedly ill mother. "Has your hired guy traced my aunt's whereabouts? Hopefully, my mother is fine. I got sidetracked with Victor's —"

"I forgot. Sorry. Friend left message warning Amorosa traveling to Atlanta."

"Alone?"

He shrugged. "Probably here already. Good thing we changed motels many times."

"Yeah, always better to keep moving. The Patels probably weren't too pleased when we left without paying our bill, but maybe we can catch them later."

Roman looked at me and spat on his hand. "Why pay? Those people never say a kind word about Roma people…no matter what."

I decided not to be confrontational, though I knew many scholars thought our people originated either from India or Egypt, hence the term gypsy, so we could be related to the Patels; but I merely said, "So when was this call I missed?"

"Hard to say. Maybe motel after we sang karaoke in bar with Chechen waitress in tight skirt."

"Oh, jeez. Do you have his number in your cell?"

"Yes, but bill's overdue —"

"And the service cut it off."

He shrugged his massive shoulders like a mischievous child. I squelched the urge to shake him.

"Did your guy say anything about my mom? Is she still ill?"

"She's not in any of the local hospitals under her maiden or married name."

"That means nothing. Most likely she wouldn't use her real name."

"Sorry, Clara, that's all I remember." Roman looked remorseful. "Many days we drank too much.

Victor's death…" He put his hand over his heart while keeping his eyes on the road as he drove.

I pushed back tears. "It's okay. I understand. I'm still out of it, too."

"One foot, then other," he said.

"Let's go pawn the stamps to get things rolling," I said. "I think a fortifying meal is a wise choice. Then we'll buy a pre-paid cell. You should call your guy, and I'll call Arthur."

I looked awful. My body felt raw, sunburned on the inside, like Victor had died yesterday, but it had been three weeks. Although the gray sadness overwhelmed me at moments and blotted out any joy, it was time to get back to the gym and sweat out my demons. Until Victor's reprehensible brother arrived, I needed to be productive.

I expected Arthur to grace us with his presence any day. Our conversation hadn't been warm, but the unsavory art dealer seemed pleased Roman and I were amenable to the job. Arthur had mentioned a contact in Atlanta who was already working on the logistical details. The undercurrent of the conversation needled at me, but I couldn't sort out why as I threw my bathing suit, sarong, and towel into my gym bag. My concerns could wait.

Before we left, Roman was fussing about dropping me off at the gym. He didn't like the new economy-sized rental car. It was unlike Roman to gripe, but grief does funny things to people. After a silent drive, I hugged his neck and thanked him for going out of his way for me. As I hopped out of the car, I saw tears rim his eyes. "I love you, Uncle."

"Yes, I know. Now, go."

Because I had skipped breakfast, I stopped by a deli in the atrium near the gym. Hernando sat by himself in a booth. I couldn't believe it. I ducked my head. As I passed through the food line, choosing a salad and an iced tea then paying the cashier, I wondered how Victor would've handled it if Roman or I had died. Recalling Victor's face, my mind wandered. I realized too late I had been standing in the middle of the dining room frozen in one spot, staring blindly out the patio sliding glass doors.

Then I saw Hernando watching me. He smiled. I felt myself blush and almost dropped my food. Before I could run away, Hernando was beside me. He asked me if I would allow him to help with my tray. He added, "I would be honored if you would join me for lunch. I always eat alone. May I?"

I nodded. My tongue stuck to the roof of my mouth. When he took my elbow and guided me to the booth, I shivered. If Hernando noticed, he discreetly hid it.

After we sat down and introduced ourselves, he ventured, "Don't you swim? I think I've seen you doing laps at the pool."

"Yes." I blushed again. He'd seen me in a bathing suit. To make matters worse, I remembered tripping Sadye in the locker room and the possibility Hernando knew the escapade was deliberate. I took a long swig of tea. "I'm sorry. You must think I'm daft. A relative…died suddenly. I'm not quite myself."

"Please, do not apologize. I see you were close to your… I am sorry for your loss, Clara.

Family is important." He paused while I took a bite of food. "But if you will permit me to say this, it is my luck that we met today." He smiled, using just his eyes. "Only a salad. Would you like to share a piece of my coconut custard pie? It's very good." He pulled out a large triangular-shaped slice from his backpack. "A nice older lady made it for me because I fixed her porch railing. Do you know what she told me?"

He waited until I answered. "I have no idea."

"That her award-winning pies make everybody happier. Let me help you smile, if only a little like Mona Lisa."

I knew Sadye had made the pie, but I couldn't resist Hernando's charming invitation. There was more to this man than eye candy.

When I returned from the gym I began a search for the intriguing Hernando Alves and found no matches on the Internet. The frustration built because I found not a trace of Hernando on social media. His address came back to an Alexandria Alves. A derivative associated with Spanish-Portuguese families in areas surrounding Castille, Spain, intrigued me. I knew the Pyrenees on the French-Spanish border as one of the common regions from where Roma travelers hailed. I grew up with tales of my people roaming near both borders. Engrossed, I barely heard Roman tell me to answer my phone.

"Hello," I grumbled into my cell without making any attempt to disguise my impatience.

"Clara, am I disturbing you?" I sat up in the squeaky desk chair. The British-accented caller didn't wait for an answer. "Arthur here. I have just arrived in Atlanta. I am being shuttled to my hotel. The American way and all that. I'd like to meet tonight."

"All right and, by the way, I'm fine, and Victor's ashes are staying with me."

There was a long pause, and then Arthur said, "Of course. Victor would've preferred you handle his affairs, etcetera. I will not haggle over his meager possessions or assets."

"You're one magnanimous, sentimental guy, Arthur. When and where do we meet?"

He coughed to cover a chuckle. "The restaurant inside the DeKalb-Peachtree Airport at seven o'clock."

"Got it. Roman and I will be there."

"Roman? Oh, right. I'm sure we can come to an agreement about who are the major players in this operation and let each of us give the proper compensation to our underlings."

Before I could object, Arthur followed the British way and rang off.

I felt horrible about what I was about to do, but I didn't have the time, patience, or money to vet Hernando in the proper way. I needed to focus on the meeting about the job tonight, and I couldn't until I put to rest whether I was going to accept an invitation to a party with my admirer. I had seen him at the gym a couple of days after the now infamous café fiasco — Roman thought the story was hilarious — and Hernando had mentioned he and his ten-year-old daughter would love it if I were their guest for the barbeque at Sadye's house on Sunday. The presence of the daughter would make our first date casual. Had Hernando sensed my MO tended to be like a skittish cat?

I parked halfway up Hernando's driveway and got out of the car carrying my purse and a book. The bushes against the chain-linked fence partially blocked the closest neighbor's view of the house. Because of Hernando's trusting nature, it was a safe bet that a door or a window was unlocked. A side window was cracked open about an inch, an option, but making entry more visible than the back door. From my previous casing of the street with Roman, I had registered the elderly neighbor on the other side of the house kept vigil; for her benefit I had worn a floppy hat and had laid the book with a generic thank you note signed with a fake name on the back steps, betting she wasn't quick enough to catch me at the back door. It opened, and I stepped inside a yellow freshly painted kitchen with new appliances and countertops with the original patina hardwood floor sanded and varnished.

I figured I had five minutes before the octogenarian snuck through her backyard to Hernando's, read the note, and registered a strange car was still in the driveway; and then another five to ten minutes before the patrol cars arrived.

Walking through the house I put on a set of gloves. I found an old address book that listed passwords in his desk. I got through on the third try and stuck a thumb drive in his computer to copy his files. I checked his stack of opened mail before I continued through the maze of rooms. The bedrooms upstairs revealed the lived-in look of a busy person. An attempt had been made to organize the bathrooms and closets, especially in the girl's room that contained pink and purple rainbows mixed with posters of pop stars and opera legends. Victor loved opera and had passed the passion on to me.

I touched Hernando's work shirts hanging in his closet. A faint tobacco aroma made me recall a childhood memory of the cigar box wherein I kept my treasures as a child. My father gave the empty box to me while I still loved him with a little girl's adoration. As I left the bedroom, I wondered if Hernando smoked.

I smelled the oil paint in the hallway before I found the studio. He was an artist. Skilled sketches positioned about the room showed images of a girl, elementary-school-aged, doubtless his daughter. A canvas was covered in the center of the room. When I peeked, it wasn't the child, but a dark Rembrandt-style portrait.

My cell alarm went off. *Time to go.* I took a shot of the portrait with my phone, collected the thumb drive, and scurried to the front door. I took a breath, removed my gloves, and imagined I was visiting with my dearest childhood friend, Barbara, before I stepped out into the sunshine smiling and waved goodbye to the air in the doorway.

As I drove away, pangs of guilt about invading Hernando's privacy made me vacillate about using his personal data to check on him further, but I didn't erase the cellphone photo of the medical document containing Hernando's Social Security number. My gut told me to hang on to the information.

6

I missed Victor for so many reasons. He enjoyed being the mastermind of our criminal endeavors, playing the game. I never paid much attention until he laid out the con and told us our roles. As a result, Roman and I had never planned a job by ourselves. We felt nervous about the upcoming meeting with Arthur. I knew the worm had his own plan in play with his Atlanta contacts, and his agenda was in his best interest. Roman and I were handy subordinates only.

I decided to record the meeting using my cell. I wanted an opportunity to weigh the nuances of the conversation later. Roman, as usual, summed up our lengthy discussion on how to handle Arthur in a concise manner. "You talk, and I back you."

I changed from my jeans, dressing in my best suit and heels and finished my lawyer look with discreet diamond-studded earrings and a designer leather handbag. Inside the vehicle, I checked my lipstick in the makeup mirror and clipped my dark hair at the nape of my neck. When Roman started the engine, he paused long enough to say, "You look hot, but not too hot. A woman to be…how you say, reckoned with."

"Thanks," I said, realizing I needed the boost of confidence. "At least I look the part. Now, let's see if I can pull it off." I slipped my sunglasses in place.

We agreed each of us would drink only one glass of wine with dinner and surreptitiously try to take a photo of Arthur's contact. Roman briefed me again because plans had changed. We weren't meeting at The Airport Café, but a restaurant on Clairemont Avenue with a reputation for authentic Mediterranean food. Built in the 1960s, it was still run by the original owners, the Greek Kontos family. Roman had checked the place during the lunch rush. There were tables in the back of a large dining room for guests who needed quiet conversation, and security cameras in the lobby entrance and outside the front and rear doors. Patio seating was available with the best view of the street, but Arthur wouldn't pick an open area to discuss anything related to business. He prided himself on being thorough. "Thank you, Roman. You're a man a woman can count on."

"No problem. Don't worry," he said. "We teach smarty pants big lesson."

As we expected, the hostess seated us in the rear of the restaurant when we mentioned Arthur. I chose the chair at the head of the table, so to speak; Roman sat on my right. Victor had taught me well. A vaguely familiar Latino man nursing a cup of coffee watched us from a booth next to the windows, but Arthur wasn't there.

Leaning toward Roman, I commented, "You notice the curious patron beside us?"

Ignoring me, he said, "I see Arthur. Look at front." Roman nodded toward the entrance as Arthur made his way to us. He wore a European tailored suit with a red tie and carried a briefcase. As he passed the man in the booth, the slim, athletic man dressed in a sports shirt and slacks stood up and followed Arthur to our table.

As Arthur neared, a wave of sorrow struck me. He was only Victor's fraternal twin, but the physical resemblance forced tears to my eyes.

"Clara, my dear, you look ravishing," Arthur said before he and his companion sat down. "What a vision. You were always a beauty, but now a grown elegant woman. Victor should be proud. Hmm," he coughed. "I'm sure he was."

When I said nothing, he filled the silence. "You think I'm a monster and believe I don't care my brother is dead. You're wrong. I loved him as only two siblings can: With passionate rivalry. Blood ties never unravel."

The waitress appeared from nowhere, filled our water glasses, confirmed our pre-arranged order, and disappeared. Apparently, Arthur had ordered what he considered a Mediterranean gourmet delight complete with the proper wine. I disliked him even more for his presumption.

"Arthur, you misjudge me." I paused. "Your passions are your private concerns, as is my grief, but I don't intend to pretend we're friends. Roman and I are here to discuss business."

"Quite. Fair enough." He smiled and took a sip of water. "By the way, this is Felipe. He will be an indispensable part of our business. Basically, he will be in charge of shutting down the power grid, disabling the alarm at our upcoming fundraising gala. We need you and your cohort to switch paintings during the chaos. You will only have thirty seconds before the backup system kicks in. Afterward, you, Felipe, and

I will go together to sell the painting, and then each of us will share our third with our outstanding partners."

When Arthur signaled the hostess, the first course arrived in a flourish created by several waiters. I wiped my hands with sanitizing liquid and tried to reengage in conversation about the job, but Arthur changed the subject.

Felipe lectured me, "It is the Spanish way for men to talk business after dinner and the women...not so much. There are other ways they support their men. Family. Home. Usually, it doesn't involve worrying their pretty little heads." He scanned my crossed legs, and I moved them under the table, but he continued to direct his distracting sexual innuendos toward me. It became tiring, and I excused myself to go to the bathroom.

While I washed my hands, I glanced up and saw Felipe's sinister smirk appear in the mirror. He was about two arm lengths away. "Ah, such a beauty. Now, be a good little girl and drop your underpants." He cocked his head. "No? Then I will do it for you." When he stepped forward, I held on to the ledge of the sink and kicked like a mule at the chauvinist. I hit his groin, a lucky shot. While he lay groaning in the floor, I snapped a couple of photographs with my cell and stepped over him. "Unless you're stupid enough to bother me again, I will not tell Roman. He would kill you."

When I returned, Roman looked relieved. We finished the third course by the time Felipe sat back down. Roman studied Felipe, who wouldn't meet his gaze. Finally, I said, "Gentlemen, I believe our business and the vying for position has concluded for this evening. Roman and I have other matters to attend to. Do not waste our time with another orchestrated dinner. As it stands, the terms aren't agreeable. We take the risks without the benefit of just compensation. Good night."

Roman handed me a stack of documents concerning Hernando's background and stood beside me as I sat at the desk in our rent-by-the-week motel room. "Before you read. Let me tell you my friend saw your mother. Her flu has gone away, and she sends love." I refrained from sharing my utter relief when I thanked Roman. He knew my history with my parents was complicated; that my father drove me away after I refused to marry at fourteen, and my mother did nothing.

"How about Aunt Amorosa?"

"Still no sign of crazy aunt in city."

"Good."

"Your *gadje's* interesting guy." Roman switched subjects. "Prisoner in Florida for forgery, but he's straight and narrow many years. Changed last name from Rodriquez to mother's family name, Alves. I think twelve years ago before he married. Check the file." He stepped into the kitchenette and brought back two mugs of coffee, which he placed on the desk. Roman continued, "Ex and mother live in Miami." Roman pursed his lips in approval. "Raised his child, a man alone, for six years."

I was impressed with Hernando's single parenting skills, something I would never be brave enough to do, but I didn't want to discuss my feeling. I said, "So he went legit, working blue collar since he married and started a family, though his life before involved forgery. Printing, platemaking, or distribution?"

"No. No." Roman sat down on the edge of the bed. "He draws, paints, and copies the art of famous painters like my country's Kandinsky."

"Of course. The master," I blinked. "The masters." The unfinished Rembrandt I had seen in Hernando's studio was beyond good. I hadn't told Roman about my furtive walkthrough at Hernando's place and it was too late to figure it out. "Tell me he doesn't have a brother in the cartel?"

Squinting, he studied me. "That's not funny joke. Romi from same prison told me Hernando's brother is dead."

"Okay. No red flags. Nothing to hamper me. I'm going on a real date, to a barbeque with Hernando and his daughter next Sunday." I clapped. "Let me guess. His daughter's name is Alexandria Alves."

"You got it, Boss." Roman slapped me on the shoulder, rattling my teeth. "You're regular Watson."

I noticed Roman had called me boss, a term reserved for Victor before now. I cleared my throat, "If Victor were here, he would correct you. Make that Sherlock Holmes. Doctor Watson was his protégée."

"That's right, 'Elementary.'" He winked at me. "Victor taught us many things."

"Bad Uncle, you're messing with me," I said, checking my beeping cell. "Let's hope most of the lessons stuck. Just received a text from Arthur. Wants to offer us a new deal."

Our date started at four in the afternoon. Hernando insisted on picking me up at our hotel and apologized when he was a couple of minutes late. His daughter's school project, due the next day, had delayed them. I could tell Hernando liked Roman, and Alexandria was charming when she asked my uncle to come with us to the party. He caught my eye.

I said, "What can I say? The young lady has asked you to be her escort. She obviously has excellent taste."

Alexandria grabbed Roman's huge hand and dragged him toward the door. Looking around, she stopped short. "Oh, you need to bring some food for the barbeque. Papa told me that's the polite thing for guests to do."

"Lexie, please, they're our invited guests. We have brought plenty," Hernando said.

Roman laughed. "It is a custom in my homeland too, but…" He shrugged. "I didn't know about party. I have only some pickled pigs' feet." He pointed to the ghastly pink sight floating inside a large jar.

"Ewww, gross," the ten-year-old said, sticking her nose near the glass. After studying the specimens, she said, "No way. I'm not eating any of those things."

At the party the food filled two picnic tables in the backyard. Sadye's daughter, LaShaska, greeted the guests, while a linebacker-sized guy manned the outdoor grill. Later I discovered he was Sadye's son. Everyone seemed congenial — too nice, in some cases. When LaShaska shook hands with Hernando, the young divorcee didn't let go of my date's hand until she introduced her preteen son, mentioned her ex several times, and then gushed praise about Alexandria's singular beauty. Testing how

Hernando would handle LaShaska, I walked toward the kitchen where Sadye was putting the finishing touches on two latticed pies. She welcomed me and then inquired if I wanted a drink. If she carried any ill will about our previous confrontations, she didn't show it.

Maybe my date set her straight. I remember when I mentioned to him that Sadye accused me of stealing at the gym a dark cloud had crossed over his face. He said, "Don't worry. Sadye will change her mind after she knows you as I do."

Attempting to let the whole incident go, I grabbed an iced tea and stood on the screened-in porch. People kept coming with more dishes of food as I watched Hernando rebuff LaShaska's sexual advances. Before I could rescue Hernando, Roman and his new sidekick, Alexandria, approached LaShaska asking questions and distracting her.

I waved to Hernando, who made a beeline for the porch. "Please, Clara, don't leave me again. That woman is unbelievable.

Does she not know Spanish men prefer to be the pursuers?"

"Obviously not, but I'll keep that in mind." I held Hernando's gaze and took a sip of tea.

"I didn't mean," his face grew anxious as he floundered, "that I'm not receptive to the right woman showing me attention, being clear, but —"

I laughed. "Relax. I understood what you meant. What did Roman ask LaShaska?"

"He asked about Sadye's pies."

"Ah, Roman is quite a cook in his own right and his timing is impeccable."

"Yes. I must thank him later." He surveyed the happy gathering. "He seems comfortable here. I like your uncle."

"Yes, he is a good listener."

"May I ask a personal question?"

I nodded.

"Roman is Russian. Right?

"So you wonder how we're related?"

"Yes, I suppose —"

"It's simple. Victor and Roman are my family because we choose to be."

"Victor?"

"He was my mentor and in many ways a father figure to me. He died recently. The relative I mentioned at the deli."

"I did not know…the dear one. I am sorry." Hernando reached for my hand and kissed it. "Your example disproves the saying that blood is thicker than water."

A warm tingle ran up my arm from his lips.

As we walked through the kitchen, I handed Hernando a glass of tea, and hoped our hands would touch. They didn't. I noticed Sadye was watching us with an amused expression. We continued into the living room. We surveyed the myriad of framed family photographs on Sadye's mantel while my blank mind searched for a topic of conversation. "When I was a teenager, Victor made me read the *Ninth Philosopher's Song*. Are you familiar?"

"No."

"Aldous Huxley added his thoughts to the proverb you mentioned earlier. I'm paraphrasing here, water is wider than blood." I lifted my glass. "I say we hopeful travelers, orphans, and misfits must agree."

He smiled and lifted his glass. "To all who are family," Hernando said as we clicked our glasses.

Amorosa sat on a folding chair outside her motel room on Memorial Drive. Her niece wasn't so clever. Following Clara and Roman from the gym to that woman's house in Cabbagetown and then to the man's house in Reynoldstown was easy. She pulled her wiry hair up and off her neck with a huge hair clip and finished a tepid free cup of coffee she got from the lobby carafe. Atlanta's local scenery, trashy like the motel, didn't inspire her, so she kept her focus on her cell searching the web and Facebook for the information she desired. She shielded her screen from the early May hot sun beating down on her face and arms. The old matchmaker stamped her feet when she spotted an image of a woman on Facebook resembling her old acquaintance, Kandace, or Kandy Le Rue from her stripper days in California. Her finger lingered over the friend request button.

Dirty waters flowed deep.

She had sold refreshments in the lobby while Kandy danced. They chatted and smoked on their breaks. The dancer loved Baby Ruth candy bars. When Amorosa needed a place to stay — during her short rebellious period of separation from the clan — Kandy offered her couch. They became friends of a sort. Amorosa cooked and cleaned while Kandy paid the rent and bought the groceries. If the dowdy Kandace on Facebook was the right person, bad blood was between Kandy and her. They'd been interested in the same comedian many years ago and had fought over the rube the last time they saw each other. She looked around for prying *gadje* eyes. None. She flapped her granny skirt long enough to let in the breeze and then pecked out a message on the keyboard and hit send. Amorosa needed to know if Sadye was Kandy's daughter.

Walking toward the hotel we chose for the meeting with Arthur, Roman caught my arm. "Do me big favor, don't go to bathroom unless I'm close by," he said. "Arthur's Felipe doesn't like to hear no." When I started to protest, Roman tipped up my chin and looked me square in the eyes. "You say nothing happened because with pleasure I'd beat Felipe to bloody pulp, but I know this man. Small penis makes for big bully."

Laughing, I said, "Okay, I get it. We watch out for each other, but I doubt the space will be big enough for anything to happen beyond your viewing range. But you're right. Felipe thinks he's a player. And he doesn't strike me as a technician. I bet he's the middleman hiring the local help and talent."

Roman nodded. "He doesn't dirty his pretty hands." Nothing got by Roman. While I had assessed the value of Felipe's black onyx pinkie ring at our last meeting, it had registered that his hands were smooth without calluses.

We arrived thirty minutes early because Roman needed to plant cameras and some extra bugs around the suite. I wore a necklace camera with audio. All the items had been purchased last year from an off-book source for a gig in Texas. "This might be overkill, but the videos will give us leverage if we need it," I said, trying to reassure myself.

Roman nodded, laying out his equipment. "Let's do it."

The suite contained a sitting room where we rearranged the furniture to accommodate a six-foot folding table. I had anticipated needing such a table to study the layout of the building for the gala, concentrating on exit strategies.

While Roman finished his surveillance project, I unpacked some white butcher-block paper, snacks, and a box of coffee. After cutting and laying the paper flat, I taped the corners down and dropped some markers in a mug.

We were ready.

 8

Felipe surveyed the room by walking through the suite and bobbing his head. Smiling as if we worked for him, he said, "What a comfortable space. Arthur will be pleased." He deposited his brown leather satchel on the table. "Arthur texted. He is delayed, an accident on I-285, but he asked me to lay out the schematics of the gallery and mark where the Hopper will be."

I wasn't amused by Felipe's entrance, but managed to remain on point. "I'd prefer to wait for Arthur. Before the details, we need a firm understanding of how the job will be divided monetarily and otherwise."

"As you wish, Clara. I'm not in any hurry. What's that delicious smell?" he asked as he reclined in a chair.

"Coffee. Help yourself." I walked from behind the breakfast nook counter and pointed to several mugs.

Roman stood by the door with his arms folded across his chest. I wondered how I was going to negotiate around his hostility toward Felipe when Arthur knocked on the door and entered. He brought croissants from a German bakery, according to the bag, and more coffee.

"Right. There's my happy crew." Arthur unbuttoned his suit coat. "Let's get started, shall we? Felipe, where are the blueprints of the building?" He leaned down to open his valise.

"Excuse me. Before we begin, Roman and I want fifty percent of the take, not a third. We are the ones running the risk of being arrested."

Felipe cursed and slammed the blueprints on the table.

Arthur ignored Felipe. "Clara, as yet we haven't discussed the details. The plan has changed. Somewhat. Can you wait until I finish showing you what I have in mind, then you can make your demands?"

"If Roman and I are switching out the painting while you and Felipe are safely playing good citizens in the background, I don't see what's to discuss."

Arthur sighed. "Please. It's not quite that simple. Let's all sit down." He took off his suit coat and draped it over the back of a chair, waiting for us to gather around the table before he spoke. "As you probably have guessed, I am more than acquainted with the gallery owners and most of the wealthy patrons on the guest list because I'm a respected art dealer."

Victor had indicated the opposite, but I kept silent.

"The gala is a fundraiser for the spinal clinic. You can be my guest, but I would like for you to consider allowing Felipe to escort you. He's already known as a wealthy bachelor who admires turn of the century works. In case you're unfamiliar with Hopper's American realism, he painted in a time when the French impressionists flourished. I have brought several brochures to help in your research."

I took the pamphlets and thanked him. "What about Roman?"

He continued his directives for me. "I suggest your cover be the young widow of a Texas oil baron. The Daughters of the Confederacy will never question your loyalty to the South or your money. I assume you can conduct a conversation about equestrian matters using an appropriate drawl after your recent Houston con."

"Dallas, but yes. How did you know?"

Victor let it slip he was in Texas during one of our rare phone conversations, and then a newspaper article about the con appeared last December in the *New Orleans Gazette*. "Victor's staged vignettes were his signature. Genius, really." He paused. "Now, about your role as a baroness —"

"Yes, already rehearsed." I slipped into my Southern drawl with a Texas twang. "An admirer of my psychic powers, a retired gentleman from the Lone Star State refined my riding skills while I took his generous donation for my favorite charity. Moi."

When Felipe snorted, Roman said, "Don't."

They glared at one another while Arthur added, "Now that's settled, Roman, you shall be a part of my personal security at the gala. On camera this will separate you from Clara if something goes wrong. My personal assistant has given you an impressive online background in corporate security. The building of false identities is one of her valuable skills. I must say with your enigmatic background, it wasn't too hard. One might think you never existed before coming to America. Oh, by the by, we handled that little green card issue."

Roman didn't thank Arthur.

I ignored Arthur's bait about Roman's background. "So Roman will have radio communication with the main security force while we exit the building?"

"That's correct."

"No guns," Roman said.

"How about a stun gun?" Arthur offered.

"I use that," Roman said.

I examined the diagram. "I see two possible exits. Here and here. How do I hide the painting as I leave?"

"The painting is sixteen by twenty. After cutting and rolling it, a large textured scarf or shawl will disguise a small tube. As backup, Roman can carry a knife, but Felipe will help you cut the painting away from the frame."

"If it goes as planned, I walk out the main entrance with it under my arm?"

"Exactly."

"I suggest we visit the gallery in disguise before the gala." I showed Arthur a photo of me in my old-lady-in-a-wheelchair getup. "Impressive," Arthur smiled, lowering his head for a moment. "Victor was a master at disguise. He taught you the tricks of the trade, but I recommend using an encrypted computer to take an online virtual tour to gain familiarity. Felipe can supply you with one. It lowers the risks you so aptly expressed in the beginning of the meeting about being spotted through surveillance cameras and facial recognition software."

"Touché. Tell me about the alarm system."

Felipe described the type of system and how the backup worked. "As Arthur already explained, you will have thirty seconds to switch the paintings. My expert hasn't been able to bypass the backup alarm without leaving a cyber trail. You must be able to cut out the original from the frame without damaging it and roll it up in the dark while Roman hangs the framed copy and I stash the original frame. The forgery will never be detected."

"Your forger is that good?" I asked.

"Yes, he is."

"Just curious," I said, "where will you discard the frame?"

"In plain sight," Felipe said, "on an easel behind a mezzanine event poster until an employee can slide it into a waste can."

Arthur said, "Some months ago, I planted a staff person who will remove the easel outside the view of the cameras after the event and then trash the frame. She also will unlock any doors we need to access."

Roman asked, "How you know this person won't talk to police?"

"Because we do," Felipe said.

Arthur interrupted, "After a short break, I'm sure Felipe will be more amenable to answering your reasonable question. If he won't, I will. One would suppose that all of us desire the same thing: to pull off the job without detection or apprehension."

"Arthur, why May 14?" I asked.

"Good question. That is the Museum Day worldwide celebration. It makes the current admin staff focus on political correctness and fundraising matters, not security issues. Everyone will be distracted managing the demands of the wealthy and privileged. There hasn't been a theft at this gallery since the 1980s, and it has caused the administration to be a bit overconfident."

Felipe moved to the couch, and Roman stood up some distance away from the table where he could see everyone in the room.

Feeling uncomfortable because he sat behind me, I swiveled in my chair and directed my question to a sullen Felipe on the couch. "Sounds reasonable," I said. "Now, to answer Roman's previous question about the staff member: Is this employee part of custodian staff or event management?"

Arthur answered, "Event management is loyal to me. She has worked for me for years as my executive secretary when she isn't moonlighting on side jobs at my request."

"If something goes wrong, the feds will search the building," I reminded Arthur. "What then?"

"She will handle it. Felipe will make a scene in the lobby while my executive assistant slash event coordinator — shall we call her Suzanne? — will remove the frame on a covered serving cart."

"Risky. Hopefully, it won't come to that."

"Quite right. She will be handing off the tube to hold the rolled-up painting at a prescribed time inside the bathroom. There aren't cameras inside the stalls. Before power is cut, can you manage to socialize in the gala's dog and pony show and conceal the tube in the shawl for twenty minutes or so?"

"I'm sure you already know I can."

"Yes, Victor loved to brag about you."

I changed the subject. "Before we go over the plan again, I need an agreement to be reached about splitting the cut." I felt Felipe's stare as Roman moved closer to me. "I want —"

"She wants fifty percent," Roman said, in a gravelly voice. "You promised Victor to help take care of Clara." Roman's looming presence finally sat down across from Arthur.

I was stunned. When was my future in connection with Victor's impending demise discussed? Did Victor know all along he was dying?

Arthur cleared his throat. "Yes, well, I should have guessed you would be privy to my brother's every thought." Arthur knew Victor was gay, something we never discussed, and Roman wasn't. However, we never acknowledged any of it because of our *marime* beliefs. I watched in angst as the men faced off in silence until Arthur said, "And I have every intention of keeping my agreement." He tipped his head at an angle. "As you wish, I will only extract my expenses and pay Felipe his third."

He had anticipated our demands, and caved too easily.

Even though I was sure Arthur and Felipe had discussed the eventuality of a new deal prior to the meeting, Felipe left the room fuming. He mumbled something about fresh air and a cigarette, not adding any curses or derogatory name-calling. The

Hopper painting was worth about eighteen million on the black market. The bully's cut would be close to six million, minus the expenses of the talent or forger and the technical crew. I calculated we would make a dent of around three million in Arthur's takeaway, but still both men would be left with a nice chunk of change. I looked forward to splitting eight to nine million with Roman, but I wondered if I was missing a crucial part of the puzzle, and it made me uneasy. The meeting was adjourned.

I was going to make more money than I had ever dreamed possible.

Exhausted from jockeying the information and personalities at the planning meeting, I opted for a walk in the rain before dinner. The raindrops felt heavy hitting my exposed face. I pulled my hoodie up closer around my face. I needed to clear my head. Usually, Roman was a comfortable companion, but not tonight. I wanted some space. I found it disappointing and disconcerting Roman and Victor hadn't confided in me before my mentor's passing. I questioned where I stood with Roman. I thought Roman and I were working as a unified team. He hadn't questioned my judgment about the current job. However, I wondered if he harbored reservations.

Perhaps I'd been too passive, accepting Victor's lead while he was alive.

The drizzling rain stopped, and I became more aware of my surroundings. I circled the old courthouse on the town square, visited the Decatur Public Library, and then lost track of where I was and wandered. A parking lot and a bank registered before I saw a mother in a yellow slicker pushing a baby stroller past me on the sidewalk. I couldn't see the baby because of the protective blanket covering the stroller seating area. The baby was safe and dry, but hidden from the world. It stuck me how hard parenting must be. I thought of Hernando and Alexandria. Keeping in check the natural instinct to protect a child and allowing them to blunder and develop independence must be daunting.

Orange and pink streaks of the setting sun broke through gray clouds as I entered a coffee shop and ordered a vanilla Frappuccino. Through the window, I watched people scurry by the shop anxious to travel home or find refuge in a restaurant for an evening meal. Some of them joined the web-browsing patrons inside the coffeehouse, and most of those bought something. I studied a tall, intense woman putting up flyers on a massive, cluttered community board as I shifted closer to read about the many venues open to local artists. Open mike was advertised as an option on Friday nights outside on the patio. On a whim, I called Hernando's cell and left a message asking him to join me for open mike night. As I jogged back to the hotel a couple of blocks from downtown Decatur, I felt lighter and confident I could handle whatever came my way. My contentment was short lived.

Aunt Amorosa ambushed me in the lobby, and I knew that meant trouble.

Aunt Amorosa smiled her best con expression and cocked her head. "You look well, Clara. I bring warm blessings from your people. They miss you."

"What people would that be? You know I no longer claim my birthright."

"That may be, but you can not run away from who you are. Without family —"

"We are nothing."

Amorosa cut her eyes at me. "I did not come all the way from Indiana to fight with you. I came to make peace. I heard about Victor. I am sorry for your grief." She lifted a small, engraved metallic pendant around her neck and kissed it. "Although I never liked him, he was good to you, and so I honored him by lighting his way to the hereafter. I lit the sacred purple, pink, and white candles."

When I said nothing, Amorosa asked, "His family should find him easily. Did he have relatives who passed on recently? I feel that he did."

"Please, I already know this con by heart."

"Not everything we tell the *gadje* is a lie." Amorosa walked in a circle around me. "You have grown cynical and cruel. My little Clara was such a sweet, loyal child."

"That is before you tried to sell me as a child bride." I blocked my aunt's path.

She faced me. "You weren't a child. A child does not run away to the fox's den and survive — without their family. You, the peach ripe for picking, weren't my doing. Blame nature. I am but a lowly matchmaker."

"Ah, yes, saving twelve- to fourteen-year-old girls from being deflowered before they marry skinny teenage boys is your calling. But I grew up and made my own choices. I don't need you." Holding up my hands, I took a breath. "In the name of the Mary saints, tell me what you want, Aunt Amorosa."

"I ask for nothing. I came to give you something." Amorosa walked in the direction of the lobby couch and presented a red hand-painted cardboard box. "It's from your mother and me, but all the women of the clan worked on it, a little here and there."

I was stunned. The incantations written on the box by the women blessed me in my forthcoming marriage. I took a step back. "I am not engaged."

"No, but you will be soon. Do you not feel an urgency to mate?" My aunt held out the heavy package.

"Is this another trick? I will never return home."

Aunt Amorosa, chubby as she was, glided across the floor in black ballet slippers and posed. Her thick bottle-black curly hair bushed out from her unpainted face accentuating the pencil-drawn eyebrows. "We have wiped away the last tears over this terrible hurt between us." She swirled her wrists the air, her bracelets clinging together, and then placed the box on a side table near me. "We accept it's the road set before us, and we travelers at heart must keep going." Amorosa gently held my shoulders. "We love you, Clara Shannesy Blythe. Please receive this gift, a celebratory quilt, to use as you wish."

I didn't trust my aunt. Where were her striped socks, mismatched floral blouse, and shapeless dress or granny skirt? She was in costume and looked like a mischievous child playing dress-up. She wore a long strand of fake pearls over a mint green vintage 1930s evening dress topped off by a silk Chinese robe displaying huge butterflies in flight participating in various forms of flower pollination. I opened the box slowly.

"We couldn't give it to you on your twentieth birthday as we wanted so we waited for the right time," she said, clasping her hands in front of her drooping breasts. "Your twenty-seventh birthday year will be a lucky year for you."

The quilt border was a chocolate brown encompassing three shades of cloth squares in blues, greens, and yellows set into twenty blocks that made up a modified Turning Twenty pattern. The dandelion theme throughout the coverlet marked my childhood obsession with dandelions. All the women of the clan had signed the quilt in ink next to a six-sentenced story about me:

We found little Clara lying in a field of yellow dandelions. She refused to leave until their heads turned white, and the seeds blew away. Her mother sang her a song about autumn and about the strong spores of the hearty flower. They traveled upon the winds, populating the earth with sprawling roots and surviving for thousands of years before humankind existed. Their roots bound the trees and other plants securely upon the earth's surface. Only when the sunset faded from the horizon, and the flowers closed their sun-kissed petals would our Clara come home to supper and bed.

It was perfect. I cried.

Amorosa kissed me on the cheek. As she departed, she said, "For you I tie the forty knots to protect against the evil eye and release the Englishman's spirit to the beyond." She laid a scrap of paper on top of the quilt. "Call me at this number, soon, if you wish to untie the knotted cloth yourself and set Victor's spirit free."

The gray sameness of the warehouse stunted my sense of reality. I rolled my shoulders, stretched my arms above my laptop, and scanned the warehouse from a dumpster-dive couch to a metal door. Four hours of reading about Edward Hopper on the Internet produced more questions than answers, and I was peckish. My stomach growled. Roman, sitting across the table from me, concentrated on his cards and played solitaire. Arthur droned on beside Roman.

Carrying bags of burgers and fries, Felipe opened the metal door, a lit cigarette hanging from his lips. I was almost glad to see him. He ignored me and dropped the food on a table inches away from Roman's beefy hands nimbly shuffling his cards.

Felipe did an about face and walked toward the restroom.

Roman continued to play solitaire on the card table situated outside the chalked floor plan marked on the warehouse floor. He only looked up when Arthur quit talking. "Okay, got it," Roman said. "You make sure I'm guarding the floor with painting of girl sewing. On the night of the party at 8:30 sharp, I go to men's bathroom and get fake painting in frame from end stall. It's inside new and improved seat-cover box."

Roman made a circle in the air with his thick index finger. "Three minutes later, blackout. I hurry back to Clara and put forgery on the wall. All this rat-in-maze stuff, I do in thirty seconds. But I have questions." He raised a ringed-clad index finger in the air. "What if someone is in bathroom, or I bump into person getting to right wall? I count thirty-five steps to wall, but where to put painting *on* wall?"

"Good questions," Arthur said, pulling some white florescent tape and night goggles from a case. "Wearing these glasses, you will be able to slip through the crowd unnoticed. Suzanne will mark the floor in front of the painting and under the four corners of the frame with small pieces of this theatrical tape that will glow ever so faintly in the dark. It's Felipe's job to cut the canvas, assist Clara, and then help you hang the forgery. Everyone needs to keep practicing using the mockup room for test runs until the timing is perfect."

Roman stood up. "But I carry the knife to give to Felipe because he must go through metal-detect machine. Will you mark knife with glowing tape?"

"No, just a dot of fluorescent paint on the tip of the grip," Felipe interjected.

I finished my computer check on a fussy detail about Hopper's life and reached for a diet soda as Arthur turned toward me. "How was your night vision on the last run?"

"Fine. Unlike this warehouse without lights, I doubt it will be pitch black because of the outer glass wall on the far side of the room." I walked to the mounted blueprints taped to a whiteboard, then pointed to the parallel, red-striped chalk lines on the concrete floor indicating a dividing wall in the middle of the mockup space. "Even with this half wall blocking the paintings from the outside lights, I should still —"

"You're probably right," Arthur said as he sat down at the table and motioned for me to join him, "but if you can accomplish rolling and stuffing the loose painting in the cylinder with your eyes closed, you can do it no matter how little light is in the room."

"Agreed. Right after we eat," I said.

Roman extended the bag of food toward me. I reached in and took a burger. "I want to try out the collapsible tube versus the regular paper tube again. At this point, both props seem awkward."

Arthur smiled and turned toward the fourth member of the team as he returned from the bathroom. "Felipe, be sure you put the knife away before you help put the painting in the tube."

"Right." Felipe threw his cigarette on the concrete and stepped on it. He stood next to Roman and extended a hand. "I would like my food now."

Roman handed Felipe the bag.

Arthur positioned his drink, burger, and fries on a paper napkin folded in a perfect triangle and spread another napkin in his lap. He watched the exchange between Roman and Felipe play out. "Felipe, please sit down. Have you added a hidden pocket to your tuxedo jacket to hold the knife securely?"

Still standing, he shuffled some hot fries in his mouth. "Your assistant, *Suzanne,* is working on it. It should be ready tomorrow for dress rehearsal."

"Very good. Now, let's agree to return to work in fifteen. We have less than seventy-two hours to place the *Girl at Sewing Machine* in a private collection."

After we discarded our lunch wrappers I said, "In a way, the painting of the girl deserves to be in a private collection, not on display in a huge gallery." I tossed my soda can in the trash bin. "Its nineteen by eighteen size suggests intimacy."

Felipe laughed. "You're a sentimentalist, Clara. I'll like what the plump seamstress painting will be worth on the black market."

"Ah," Arthur said, "money is our ultimate goal, but also, I agree with Clara. The realism of Hopper inspires. Mary Leader's poem, by the same title as the painting, exists because the young woman depicted appears so at ease working alone in her room. The viewer is a voyeur. The beauty of concentration needs no company." Arthur pointed toward the mockup of the gala space. "Shall we continue?"

I didn't sleep well. Sitting at the breakfast table, I realized I was grumpy as I thanked Roman for preparing a meal I couldn't eat.

"What's wrong?" Roman asked as I stirred my coffee.

"Nothing, really. I feel I should call Aunt Amorosa today and meet her, but I still don't know what I want to do. On one hand, Victor was agnostic, and I don't really believe in warding off evil or unbinding spells although —"

"You want to honor Victor by undoing knots, so do it." He shrugged. "Then go. Your aunt's just pain in butt."

"You're right. It's closure, a ritual for the living. I am a big girl, and I can leave whenever I want."

Roman grinned. "And if you need me, call. I break down door, find Tinkerbelle."

"Why don't you come with me?"

"I don't fit so good with spoiled Americans on vacations. They live in one place and their children are soft. Besides, your aunt is pushy woman. I don't like."

I studied Roman. His so-called logic didn't hold up because we lived in motels and hotels. He was holding something back in his dark eyes. He had been going out alone on our infrequent nights off or in the late afternoons dressed as if he had a date. Respecting his privacy, I didn't ask why. Instead, I nodded and leaned in, giving him a hug. "Okay, I'll see you when I get back. Don't do anything exciting without me."

With bluegrass music playing in the background, I sat in the understated parlor that served as a lobby for a bed and breakfast in Stone Mountain, Georgia. Why would Aunt Amorosa choose such a place to stay? She loathed country folk and Southern charm. She probably had a scam going involving Old Money in the city, a place known for Sherman's overnight stay before he raided Atlanta during the Civil War. Of course most history books failed to mention the Ku Klux Klan burned crosses spearheaded by their Grand Wizard, a Venerable, and conducted ceremonies atop the granite mountain until the late fifties.

Although waiting for Amorosa irritated me, the antique couch was green brocade and stuffed hard with horsehair, the way I preferred, and the coffee the proprietor poured was the perfect temperature with real cream. I relaxed.

No doubt Aunt Amorosa would make her grand entrance soon.

The irony of the situation wasn't lost on me. In the past, the Klan in Indiana hadn't made life pleasant for any Roma families, including my relatives. The allure of a craft festival allowing palm reading might have seduced Amorosa to Stone Mountain, but only setting up a big score would keep her here. I couldn't be the only reason she had come to Atlanta.

Amorosa never showed up, but a delivery kid on a bicycle stopped by with a small box containing the coiled velvet streamer with forty knots. After I signed for the package, the pimple-faced preteen — as directed by my aunt — told the owner I would settle Amorosa's bill. I must admit some admiration for her brass pair.

Laughing, the proprietor's potbelly shook as he took my cash and nimbly swept away all traces of my coffee.

It was time to leave.

 10

Roman always could sway me. Sitting in the motel kitchenette, the smell of garlic butter heavy in the air, I watched my uncle excuse himself from our late lunch and head toward the bathroom with a new spring in his step. Our "little talk" had gone his way.

A new reality had unfolded: Roman was dating Sadye. I couldn't wrap my head around the news. He and Sadye wanted to come with Hernando and me on Friday night for open mike at the coffee shop. I hadn't flat out said no, my first inclination, but it took an awkward few minutes of rambling for me to arrive at "I want alone time with Hernando." I proposed a deal that included we would arrive in separate cars, keep our alcoholic beverage consumption to a minimum, and part ways after the performance ended.

Roman left the bathroom door open a few inches, and I heard him swishing water in the basin, no doubt shaving his heavy beard. Modesty prevented him from removing facial hair or stripping to his undershirt in front of me. He said, "I tell you not to worry. I have good feeling it goes smooth as silk at gala next week." He stepped out putting on a suit coat, and then straightened his collar in the full-length mirror on the back of the closet door.

As I removed the spaghetti and salad plates and stacked the dishes in the dishwasher, I laughed at myself about my negative reaction to the idea of a double date. I felt euphoric about the opportunity to see Hernando again. Scary stuff. I tried to picture Roman feeling this giddy about Sadye, but the image nauseated me. Finishing the last few drops of wine in my glass, I realized I hadn't altered my opinion about the woman, who must be in her early fifties, not closer to sixty as I had first thought. I preferred to think of Roman, who recently turned forty-seven, with his usual — bombshell waitress. Not a pie-baking busybody. But needs change. Yesterday, I had caught him, disgustingly happy, humming as he had tried out what I knew now was Sadye's zucchini bread recipe.

Roman kissed my head, rinsed his hands, raised the last of the cold pasta from the strainer to his mouth, and waved goodbye. He was en route to the farmers' market, one of his favorite places to explore.

"I am a lucky woman," I yelled over my shoulder.

He turned and winked at me. "Yes, I love you too, Tink," he said and shut the door.

Keeping my expectations in check, I chose a simple skirt and blouse combo for the upcoming date. Only two more days; I could hardly contain my excitement. I decided to book a pedicure and manicure for tomorrow. Low funds be damned.

The evening air was scented with citronella candles dotting the metal round tables on the open patio. I spotted a tiny stage tucked in a corner of the garden as Hernando touched the small of my back, pulled a chair out for me, and handed me a single red rose.

"Oh, my, how did you hide this beautiful flower?"

"I have my secrets," he said, displaying a tiny water capsule in his jacket pocket.

As I smelled the rose, satisfaction grew on his face. "I'll go find us some drinks. Would you like cappuccino? Glass of wine?"

"Cappuccino, please."

He nodded, and I caught a hint of his aftershave in the air as I looked up at him. "Thank you so much, Hernando."

He took my hand and kissed it. "You're welcome, Miss Clara." I felt myself blush as he penetrated my cool façade with his intense brown eyes.

I recovered my poise by the time he returned, and we listened to a band playing in the corner. A cool breeze wafted around my skirt as the bass and guitar musicians played a jazzy tune. We talked about his precocious daughter singing at a family gathering and his hope for her to attend Julliard. The concerned father role suited him; his eyes lit up whenever he spoke of his gifted Alexandria. He asked me about my life. I was about to spin an entertaining tale, a plausible lie, when Roman and Sadye arrived.

Roman nodded, but Sadye took the lead. "Hernando, there you are. I haven't seen much of you lately. My daughter, LaShaska, asked me to say hey for her."

Hernando stood until Sadye sat down. "Please convey my regards to your daughter and her son." Turning his attention to Roman, the men shook hands. Hernando said, "Good to see you, Roman. Alexandria wants you to drop by the house soon. She has a new piece she wants to perform especially for you."

"Let me know when it's good time. Your daughter, she's beyond belief, a sweet *ahern*…an angel."

"I won't fake modesty. I am a proud parent, and I thank you for your compliments."

An awkward silence ensued. I said, "Sadye, I like your necklace and earrings. Did you buy them in the Decatur area?"

"Aren't they gorgeous? LaShaska made them for me for my birthday. I wear them on special occasions." She reached across and squeezed Roman's arm. "He is my special occasion."

Roman beamed.

I wondered how many bakeoffs Uncle Roman hadn't bothered to mention to me as Sadye talked about them signing up for a couples cooking class.

After a sip of coffee, I engaged in a coughing fit. Roman shot me a scowl. Excusing myself, I sprinted for the restroom.

Everything Sadye did or said irked me. I needed a break.

After checking the restroom stalls, I made sure I was alone before I talked to myself. "What is it about this woman that annoys you so much, Clara? Victor would remind you to look at the things you dislike in yourself to gain understanding."

I took a deep breath. On my way back to the table, I paused to read the community bulletin board. While pondering whether the boy band or the improvisational theatre company flyers merited my wandering attention, I smoothed my skirt and realized I only needed to keep my mouth shut through the open mike performances, an hour tops, and then Roman and his cooking queen would leave Hernando and me alone to explore Decatur. This night was my night. I was determined to enjoy it.

I plastered a smile on my face and approached our table as I heard Sadye say, "Thank you, Hernando, we would love to go back with you all to your house. I'll finally get to see your place and your paintings. Did you know he paints, Clara?"

I couldn't remember if Hernando had told me about his art, or if I knew because of my unauthorized tour of his home, but I managed to say, "I think he mentioned a painting of Alexandria. Am I right?"

Hernando nodded, but I could tell he hadn't mentioned any such thing to me.

★ ★ ★ ★ ★

As I darted from the piano to the mantel in Hernando's living room, I wondered if he would confront me about my slip of the tongue. "Where's Alexandria?" I asked, not sure where to put my hands as I walked to the window.

Hernando grinned and dropped his gaze. "Remember. She is at a sleepover birthday party. The girl's parents are old friends of mine. Please, let's sit down."

I remained standing near the window watching dark clouds gather in the sky while Roman and Sadye sat on the couch.

"What's wrong, Clara?" Hernando said and sidled up next to me. "Why don't you sit down, and I will bring you some wine. Relax, you look beautiful." He hugged me and headed toward the kitchen.

Sadye blabbered nonstop about whatever floated through her brain, and I wandered around the room as the full impact of having broken into this decent man's house weighed on me.

The spring rain hit the gutters outside. I was only half listening, but I heard Sadye express her praise for the oak staircase and a portrait of Alexandria hanging over the fireplace. When she launched into a long tale about her cooking awards, Roman's delight grew.

She finally wrapped it up. "My first blue ribbon for baking was for a German chocolate cake when I was sixteen. I added a dash of hot sauce to my grandmother's recipe to win the Future Farmers of America baking contest at the 1977 Kansas City Expo." Glowing, Sadye turned to Roman. "I will make it for you, my Roh-Man, as soon as I buy some fresh walnuts on my way to Savannah. I'm picky about my ingredients and my men."

Roman practically cooed.

Before I could comment about Sadye's mispronunciation of Roman's name, Sadye asked, "Do you cook?"

"I can't boil water," I said, exaggerating my lame kitchen skills.

The doorbell rang.

Hernando answered the door and ushered a male figure into the living room. I couldn't see the new arrival's face clearly until he took off the hood of his drenched raincoat.

"Hey everyone. I want you to meet my brother, Felipe," Hernando said.

Sadye and everyone else smiled and spoke. Me? I couldn't seem to breathe.

Roman saved the day by shaking Felipe's hand as if they'd never met, and there hadn't been conflict between them. I managed to nod toward a smirking Felipe as my date excused himself to retrieve refreshments.

We stared at each other for a few seconds before Roman took Sadye's hand, suggesting they watch the storm from the rocking chairs on the front porch. They left Felipe and me alone.

"What are you doing here?" Felipe said, pushing the coffee table several inches in my direction with the toe of his shiny dress shoe.

"I am on a date. I didn't know —"

"That he is my brother and the talent for our little shared enterprise?"

Again, I was speechless as I realized Hernando must be the painter, the forger, for our operation.

How could I have been so blind?

"This is only our second date," I stammered, as Hernando re-entered the room with a tray. "My first invitation into his lovely home. I didn't know…Hernando had a brother."

"How did you meet?" Felipe asked.

Hernando handed his brother a drink. "We met at the gym where I work. Please, stop questioning Clara as if you're the Grand Inquisitor."

"What are the chances," Felipe shrugged and continued, "that you would find such a beauty at the gym? Amazing."

"One in a million, but I am glad I did. My Alexandria approved of Clara at first sight. This woman left quite an impression by reading your niece's palm. Oh, I'm sorry, Clara is a psychic."

"A psychic." Felipe nodded. "No doubt a woman of many hidden talents."

"I believe dogs and children are rarely wrong," Hernando said, reaching for my hand. "Besides, one must take a chance for love to bloom."

It was too much. Excusing myself, I started to gather my things. "I'm so sorry, but I'm not feeling well."

"Wait. I will walk you out," Felipe said. He stood and approached me, holding up a hand toward Hernando's protests.

"Considering your divorce, Hernando, perhaps you're not an authority on relationships, and as luck provides, I already know Miss Clara very well. I think you should know a bit more about this grifter." Felipe held my gaze. "Would you like to tell him, or should I?"

"What is happening?" Hernando said, turning toward me.

Words wouldn't form in my mouth.

Roman's voice boomed through the room as he entered. "Shut up, Felipe. You insult my Clara. She doesn't need to explain. *You* involve your brother in our business." Roman studied Felipe. "I think you're stupid man." His pursed lips spat out the word, "*Gadje.*"

Roman looked at me. "We go."

With my head held high, I left without saying goodbye.

Realizing Roman felt responsible in this fiasco of identifying brothers, I said, "As my Scottish grandmother would say, 'This is either one fine calamity, or it's for the best.' Both of us have been distracted. Victor's death and our romances have us off our games." I took a breath in and exhaled, counting to eight trying to control my sense of loss.

Roman nodded.

"Anyway, almost everything is out in the open between Hernando and me. That's good." I turned around, scanning the empty backseat. "Where's Sadye? Did we leave her behind?"

"I called Sadye a cab when you talk with Felipe. Not good for her to hear stuff." He pulled the car into a strip mall parking lot and stopped. "Besides job, what's not out in open?"

"Before our first date, I went through Hernando's house on my own, and I should've put two and two together about his forgery skills."

Roman cut his eyes at me.

I ventured into unsafe waters as I said, "So during your vetting process, I don't blame you for not catching that Felipe and Hernando are brothers."

"You throw vetting Hernando in my face when you...Clever girl." He made a brushing away motion with his hands. "You cased inside of house without me, broke our rules, and spied on man you want for lover?" Roman shrugged. "Both of us fucked up."

"Yep, big time."

Roman laughed. "I bet Arthur has plan to double-cross us, but Felipe, maybe, plan to double-cross everybody."

"Leaving us screwed either way."

"Big time, unless smart boss turn table around."

★ ★ ★ ★ ★

Roman handed me the heavy fabric, squeezed my shoulder, and closed the motel door leaving me with my thoughts. He understood I wished to conduct the untying ritual for Victor on my own. Aunt Amorosa's words replayed about the importance of easing the departed one's spirit from this earthly plane to the next. Minutes ticked away, but I couldn't make my hands move until I heard soothing classical music coming from an open window. Antonin Dvorak's *Symphony No. 9 – Largo* ½ was music I recognized. I'd heard it in the funeral scene of the movie "Clear and Present Danger", and Victor had taken that opportunity to school me in great Czech composers.

I realized Roman must've been listening to the car stereo with the windows down. With shaking hands I untied the forty knots binding the dark blue velvet strip. I let my tears fall on the soft material. The color and texture reminded me of Victor's smoking jacket and his genteel style. I missed him, and I wished I could tell him about Hernando. As the fabric piece became longer and longer, remembering my mentor never refused me anything outright, I smiled.

One of my first disagreements with Victor had pertained to the allure of nightlife and romance. I must've been shy of fifteen and determined to go clubbing with a guitarist, a young man at least ten years older than myself. Victor the Great, as I called him when I was miffed, suggested that a musician in his twenties would want his girl to hold down a stable job, "bring in the bacon" as the Americans say, and then eventually become his wife. I went anyway.

My date talked about himself all night, asked me to pay for the drink tab while calling me "his girl". I ditched the boring guy at the club by excusing myself for a restroom break, circling back to the front door, and taking a taxi back to my carefree life with Victor and Roman.

There were no reprisals on that long-ago night. In our pajamas, my associates and I had raided the small refrigerator we kept full of delicacies, such as Russian caviar, and watched an old movie starring Ginger Rogers. I laughed at Victor's antics describing Fred Astaire's manic dance-until-you-drop rehearsals. Of course, Victor told us he had known someone — who would remain nameless — who had an affair with Ginger's pianist. Later, as I drifted to sleep on the couch, I felt one of my companions kiss me on the forehead and cover me with a blanket.

Beside me the unknotted crinkled cloth lay on the table. I stretched the three-yard strip out to its full length and width. I grabbed a black marker and listed on the backside of the material many of my treasured memories and mementos Victor had bestowed on me, and then I took my friend's walking stick, his funeral urn, and matches outside along with a bottle of vodka and a glass. Sitting inside the idling rental car, Roman watched me walk behind the motel toward the woods, but he didn't follow. I hummed a melody from Chopin's *Piano Concerto No. 2* as I gathered leaves and sticks for kindling, struck a match, and observed white flames consume the velvet.

A burnt paper scent filled the air.

Picturing Victor I raised a glass in celebration and resisted the temptation to hold fast to my dear friend's essence. I forced myself to scoop the smoldering ashes into the lid of the urn.

"This next part will be a bit dramatic but so fitting for you, Victor," I said, spreading my arms and pronouncing my benediction: "I let go. I release you. Travel on safely, my dear Impresario."

I felt at peace while I emptied the urn. Using Victor's walking stick to scatter the ashes at the base of an oak tree, I prayed for a good audience wherever his spirit landed.

I watched Hernando pace in front of the gym. We had spoken on the phone to set up this face-to-face meeting, but neither of us had revealed our emotions concerning Felipe's bombshell. I parked without a clue of what to say to Hernando. He rushed toward me as I climbed out of the rental car. Struck by his broad shoulders, dark hair, and athletic physique, my attraction to him overwhelmed me. Extending his arms, he said, "Clara, you must believe me I had no idea you or Roman were involved. Felipe tells me what to paint, I do it, and he pays me."

I motioned for Hernando to lower his voice and searched the parking lot for onlookers.

Continuing with less volume, he said, "I never know if a dealer wants the copy to pass off to a collector, or if it's part of —"

"A heist," I whispered in his ear, and then held his gaze. "Apparently, both you and I make the major portion of our income beyond the boundaries of the law while we pretend to do otherwise."

He took my hands. "Do you believe me?"

"Yes, if you can believe I didn't know you were Felipe's brother."

"Of course. You and I just happened to meet." We exchanged glances. It sounded absurd when stated out loud. I could see him struggle to put his doubt aside. He placed our hands together on his chest for a moment. "You aren't upset with me?"

"No, but don't you think we were too good at fooling ourselves and each other?" I cleared my throat. "I guess we should remain professional and not see each other until after the job," I said, regretting every word.

He focused on our hands, brushing my knuckles with his fingertips. "Yes, I suppose we should, but you will move on, and I'll never see you again." His shoulders sagged and his handsome face transmitted deep sadness. "I will miss you."

For a moment we smiled at each other, and he kissed me. I steadied myself against the car and watched Hernando turn and walk away.

My stomach was queasy but I acted delighted to be in the backseat of a limousine with Felipe, a man playing his debonair bachelor role to the hilt. The pre-performance butterflies in my stomach were normal for me. Victor considered each con a performance where the audience participated in the ultimate outcome, determining whether a drama or comedy unfolded.

Warming up my Southern drawl during the drive to the gala, Felipe and I intentionally quarreled, giving the driver an earful. If a problem arose, the contingency plan included that I would leave without my escort, feigning another flareup between lovers.

When I stepped out of the limo with Felipe at the gala, I focused on playing my part. I became Miss Lillian "Lily" Wentworth. My full-length couture dress, blue-sequined with long sleeves, shimmered in the headlights of the limousines lined up behind us waiting for valet service.

I had chosen the dress for practical reasons. I might need the thin stretchy sleeves to stabilize the retractable tube under the satin shawl, but the fabric and cut felt luxurious. Walking up the steps, the front split in my dress revealed enough leg to capture interest.

In character as the gala's curator and fundraiser, Arthur nodded his approval and flirted just enough with me, now the Texas oil-millionaire heiress, while ushering us inside the marble-walled atrium and into a roped-off elevator.

When the elevator doors opened upstairs onto the fifth floor, I saw beautiful people everywhere. A string quartet provided soothing background music that encouraged the guests to mingle, to hide their competitiveness, and to remain polite.

Tonight was a night to be generous, or at least act gracious.

With me on his arm, Felipe walked around the exhibition hall gladhanding as he introduced me to the right people. I shook hands with bankers, CEOs of Fortune 500 companies, and an array of famous athletes, college chancellors, and politicians. The spouses of these men watched their husbands scan my body, and then plastered their Stepford-wives' smiles on as they dragged their powerful men away to the other side of the room.

The exhibition hall contained three enormous chandeliers reminding me of the Yellow-Button Chandeliers found in Frank Lloyd Wright's home. The exquisite lighting for each painting, the crown molding, and the off-white walls offset the diffused overhead lighting. While we worked the room, I mentally checked on the accuracy of the warehouse mock-up. Everything seemed the same, including the placement of the security cameras and Hopper's painting of the placid red-hued *Girl at Sewing Machine*. Struck by its beauty, I almost missed Roman in his Secret Service-like getup standing in a corner with an earpiece, clean shaven, and sporting short-cropped hair. The military haircut and shave had been big sacrifices he'd made to make millions. When he spoke into the cuff of his sleeve, I almost lost it and covered my mouth to hide my laugh.

Felipe shot me a warning glance and tapped his Rolex. "Would you like another drink, Lily, before the auction begins? Or you, Martha?" Felipe asked the woman with a diamond ring the size of a quarter.

The bejeweled woman nodded. "I am thirsty. Apparently, my Harry has vanished in pursuit of libations or whatever. He left ages ago."

"I must visit the Ladies room," I said, "but you two indulge without me." Guests blocked my way, so I circled Felipe and Martha searching for a clear path.

"A wonderful idea," Martha said, patting Felipe's chest. "Don't you just adore

Hopper's landscapes, such a slice of Americana, painted in a time when the impressionists were blurring the lines? Not that I don't like to blur a few lines myself."

I couldn't resist. I tipped my head between them. "Of course, Martha, y'all know I'm only speaking of drinks." I laughed as middle-aged Martha's mouth gaped. "Now don't get lost, you handsome thing," I said, tugging at Felipe's sleeve.

While my date swept the chatty CEO's wife toward the bar, I walked through the crowd and entered the Ladies restroom.

It was showtime.

A busty matron, preparing to leave the restroom with a cleaning caddy in hand, blocked me. "If you're the woman that complained," she said, "I just placed a box of new seat covers in stall five."

I nodded. The housekeeping staff member was blond–haired Suzanne,

Arthur's assistant, and the seat cover information a ruse. Roman and I had been provided a photograph of Arthur's assistant at the mock-up site. It did her justice, but didn't define her height. She towered over me. Besides making me feel small, she was a question mark, and I didn't like unanswered questions. While gauging her Norwegian characteristics as six-foot and large-framed, I thanked her. She would be a hard one to take down in a fight.

I found what I sought, stuck on the wall of stall five. Suzanne had painted the compacted tube — now about the diameter of a hamburger — industrial dark beige, and then wedged it near a back corner. Ripping off the matching painter's tape, I tucked the tube inside a sleeve, covered it with my shawl, and left.

I checked my cell. Right on schedule. The lights would go out in fifteen minutes. Before I could slip through the throng of tuxedoed and couture-gowned guests, each trying to impress each other, and find Felipe, the master of ceremonies hushed the crowd. Arthur stepped forward to introduce the guest artists. "I present a special treat. A young soprano, Miss Alexandria Alves, accompanied by her father, Hernando Alves, on classical guitar."

I stared at Arthur standing in the center of the stage under a glistening chandelier. He returned my gaze with a laser focus and nodded.

What the hell?

Roman passed by me on the outskirts of the throng and pulled his ear — his signal for an emergency meeting. If we did nothing, Alexandria might recognize Roman or me. As I headed toward the nearest stairwell, I began to think of alternate means of escape in case this caper went south.

I had anticipated Arthur or Felipe absconding with the painting or the money once the Hopper had been stolen, making us patsies after the fact, but why would they alert us by placing a kink in the plan, unless

Alexandria was a distraction to put Roman and me off our games?

Roman was moving toward me, but then he turned abruptly toward the exit sign. I followed.

My uncle gave me a bear hug in the stairwell. After he released me, he said, "At big security briefing this morning, I told about Alexandria singing, but no way to tell you. What's our plan, Boss?"

I said the first thing that came to mind. "I don't like it. Do you agree it feels like a train speeding toward a brick wall?"

"Boom," he said, smashing one palm against the other.

"We could stay with the original plan and play it out, leave flat broke right now, or when the lights go out, we go to plan B. You replace the original with the fake as expected, I take the real painting and meet you in the kitchen, and then we run for it. What's your choice?"

"We take Hopper. Cut out other guys."

"I'll meet you ASAP in the kitchen?"

"Yes. Good thing I memorized streets around museum and thought of way to catch train." Roman handed me a city railway pass card. "Just in case. Turn right. Go two blocks. Train on your left."

I repeated the directions. "You're a genius, Uncle, and I bet you already stashed a car in one of the transit parking lots."

"You know it. Our suitcases are in trunk at Chamblee Station. You take car-door opener." He fished inside his pocket. "Look for a white Malibu in E-6."

"Very good." I took the key fob. "Now, let's get back to this party and make it go our way. We're leaving this conniving crew to their own devices."

Roman caught my hand. "Be careful, Clara. Remember Felipe's knife. You take my Taser."

I took the Taser without argument. A move I'd regret.

After Alexandria and Hernando had left the stage, Roman headed toward the men's bathroom to retrieve the fake painting, and I positioned myself near the Hopper painting, but I couldn't locate Felipe. The jerk waited until the last possible second to approach from behind. Felipe squeezed my shoulders. "Nervous, my pet?"

I said, "You're a bad boy," trying to sound unruffled. "Involving Alexandria and Hernando was risky. Why?"

"The sweet star-to-be talked Hernando and me into allowing the gig because the patrons of the arts, big money, are here to hear her sing. Contacts are so important to a prodigy. Don't you agree?"

I huffed.

"Don't worry. After she sang her last perfect note, Hernando swept her away."

"I would hope so," I said. "The child doesn't need to be in the middle of...a job."

"Do I sense motherly concern? How attractive." Felipe touched my face, and I flinched.

"What's done is done. Let's get back on task," I said.

"Of course, I —" Felipe's cell rang. Accepting the call, he covered his other ear, blocking the cacophony in the room. "A problem. How much longer? Cut that in half."

As Felipe assured me that everything was under control, I surmised the tech guy on the other end of the conversation wasn't having a good night, and we were running out of luck.

"How much longer?" I said.

"Ten."

"I'll call Roman."

"No," Felipe said.

"Excuse me. You aren't in charge here."

He took my hands and rubbed my knuckles, not unlike Hernando during our last rendezvous. I shivered. "I suggest you calm yourself, and I'll call Arthur."

Behind me, I heard, "Did someone call my name? I am at your service." Arthur slid between us and gestured toward the lavishly clad people roving from one cluster to another, laughing and slapping each other on their backs. "Isn't this night electric?"

Holding a white-toothed smile, Felipe said, "A problem, a computer glitch on the lights. The tech needs ten more minutes."

Arthur shrugged. "We wait."

I said, "Do something. Roman is already in the bathroom."

"Bloody bad timing," Arthur replied. "Oh, well, since improvisation is your forte, Clara, we shall follow your lead and play the cards as they're dealt. Be alert. I'm sure Roman will wait until the lights go out to make his move."

13

When the lights went out, I uncoiled the tube as Felipe cut the painting from the frame. I felt Roman pinch my waist in the dark, our sign that all was going according to our clandestine plan. I rolled and inserted the valuable painting in the cylinder. When the lights came back on the gathering became quiet, and then the puzzled patrons of the arts burst into a roar, a chaotic mixture of complaints and exclamations. Felipe, our untrustworthy accomplice, disappeared. The fake painting glistened in the overhead gallery spotlights. My heart pounded. The girl sewing in the red-hued painting personified self-contentment. For a moment, I envied her. Nobody would ever guess she was a forgery. Hernando was a genius.

"May I offer you a glass of Champagne?"

I spun around. The gala ballroom seemed to whirl around me. "Hernando, what a surprise. The second time tonight you have caught me unaware."

Roman disappeared outside my peripheral vision as Hernando continued. "I apologize if Alexandria and I upset you by performing tonight. I could tell by your hasty retreat out of the room that you were troubled, but I hope not because you were unhappy to see me."

"Under the circumstances, I don't know. I must admit I wondered why you and Felipe would jeopardize our objectives for this evening and place Alexandria in a compromising situation. What if she had recognized Roman or me and called out to us?"

Hernando looked as if something was lost in translation. "Surely you knew Arthur approached my family and cajoled us. Of course, my little songbird was overjoyed to perform for the fundraiser."

I waited, arms folded.

"In lieu of payment, her fee will be sent to a charity sponsoring artists with disabilities." He combed his hands through his hair. "Please. I never left my daughter's side. Alexandria was told to sing, leave the stage, and speak to no one. She knows once my trust is broken, I do not forgive easily."

As his words struck home and the stolen painting shifted inside my sleeve, I felt the weight of my decision to double-cross Arthur and Felipe. Roman would be in the kitchen waiting for me to bring the painting.

I had to go.

Underneath my shawl I tucked my arm with the Hopper masterpiece in its tube against my chest as I bent to kiss Hernando's cheek. "Maybe, you're for real. Who knows? What I see is a crazy talent and possibly even a good man, but I'm in a bad situation. Someday, I hope you'll understand." I walked away.

An alarm sounded as Roman and I exited through the kitchen doorway into the alley. Suzanne, at least a foot taller than Roman, came around the far corner of the alley yelling for us to stop. She sprinted past a security officer flanking us on the left. He had a gun or Taser. We ran in the direction of the railway station with both of our pursuers less than twenty-five feet behind us. When I was close to the turnstiles, Roman yelled, "Split pea." At his reference to the old shell game misdirect, I acted like I passed the Hopper to him, and he broke off and turned right. I knew he was hoping to divert our chasers from the painting and me. It worked, but I glanced back to see Suzanne and the huge security guy lunge for Roman and take him down. They rolled out of the streetlight illumination.

I remembered Roman didn't have the Taser. I did. I climbed the stairs two at a time and lifted a navy hoodie from a college student's tote bag as I passed by. As I reached the platform with my heart racing in my chest, I slipped on the hoodie trying to conceal my face and slow my breathing. I grabbed at the cloth near my front kick pleat and tied the two front panels of my gown together at thigh level.

All I could do was keep going. The train doors opened, and I hurried inside a car. The train doors closed as Suzanne topped the escalator, and I watched her figure become a blur as the train cars left the station. My partner had either let himself be caught, or he had fought his way free. I wondered if the authorities were en route, or if Arthur intervened. Roman would never tell the *gadje* a thing, and after an inventory of the museum showed nothing missing, they would have to let him go…I hoped.

Felipe paced inside the glass conference room and Arthur negotiated a price for the muscle-bound security officer's silence concerning Roman's capture. Security's jacket pocket was dangling by a corner, the only casualty from the fight with the Russian inside the Arts Center Transit Station entrance.

Security had delivered Roman to the basement and handcuffed him to an iron pole. Arthur departed with Security, leaving Felipe alone with the captive. He hit Roman in the face until he broke his nose and slid down the pole. Felipe kicked him in his ribs, catching a kidney. Roman doubled over and leaned to the side gasping for breath.

"Brave man beats on handcuffed man. You're a coward." He spat on the floor and curled his bleeding lips into a grin.

Felipe backhanded Roman and raised a chair over his head as somebody ran down the stairs.

"Stop it," Suzanne yelled and pulled the chair away from Felipe. "We need him alive. Lose control and lose the prize."

"Go fuck yourself," Felipe said. "You let Clara get away."

She grunted. "I should've known. Remember, jerk. I found you down for the count in the stairwell."

Felipe envisioned choking her long skinny neck. He popped his knuckles.

She checked Roman's pockets. "Where is the Taser? He could've taken at least one of us out even without the Taser during the fight," she said, "but he didn't. Guess he was buying time for Clara to get away."

"That bitch, Clara, has it."

Arthur coughed and opened the conference door, bringing Felipe back from his reverie. "Please escort Security from the building," Arthur said. "He is no longer in our employ."

Holding in his fist his bribe of five thousand in cash, Security smirked and regarded Felipe with disdain. "Heard big Roman coldcocked you with a fire extinguisher in the stairwell. Too bad you missed the little chase and catch near MARTA. It was fun and profitable."

Felipe clenched his fists. His phone beeped and before he could stop himself he punched the conference room wall.

Arthur took a step back.

The security guy eyed the hole in the wall and took off like the Road Runner, tucking his bribe inside his blazer. He made a beeline for the elevator and kept his broad back at an angle to Felipe.

Felipe muttered a half-ass apology to Arthur and followed Security into the mezzanine. As the guy waited for the elevator, he crossed his beefy hands in front of his crotch and appeared to size up Felipe, who took a step forward as the elevator doors opened with a sharp ding.

The big guy's eyes flooded with fear while he backed into his escape hatch. Felipe stared at him until the elevator doors shut. When the ex-employee got greedy, wanted more money, or threatened to betray them, he would kill the big mouth and finish the job Arthur was too weak to do now.

As Felipe turned back toward the stairs leading to the basement, he decided he wasn't finished repaying Roman, or Clara, and he would retrieve the painting, the big score, no matter the cost.

14

After she hung up from talking to Kandy, Amorosa called her brother Bill. "That's right. She remembered me. We forgave each other."

"You were always lucky." Bill's voice sounded like gravel being walked on.

"I lit the blue candle of healing before I called her. She verified she has a daughter named Sadye Mitchell in Atlanta. Apparently, the child never knew her father, and the grandmother raised her because Miss *Can Dance* ran off with a salesman at fifteen."

"Are they on speaking terms?" he asked.

Amorosa waited to answer while he hacked up something from deep in his lungs. His pneumonia didn't sound any better than the last time she called. "Off and on. Have you been taking your antibiotic?"

"Yes, but now I have the shits."

"Keep taking the pills. When I get home I'll make you a drink of tomatoes, clivers, and mullen. Maybe dandelion root, too. It won't hurt."

"Tastes like hell though."

Amorosa laughed. "I mix in a dash of honey, baby brother."

"That sounds better. What about the rich Stone Mountain lady who believes you can help her stay in touch with her dead son?"

"It's still in play, but I'm worried about Clara. Sadye has a checkered past to say the least, and that Russian Romi is infatuated with her. Her son owns a barbershop. No telling what else he is up to. Of course, I already told you Arthur is in town. I spit over my shoulder." She spat twice into the air. "And not out of respect for Victor's passing, not that man, but because he wants something from our Clara. I feel it in my bones she is mixed up with dangerous people. I have said the new moon ritual for Clara and other family members for years —

Leave us with money. Leave us with good health. Leave us with love — but I should perform a protection spell tonight. May a juniper tree grow along her path to shield her from the hunter's arrow. I must stay here until I know she's all right."

I arrived at the Chamblee transit station and hoped for a phone call from Roman. After pulling on a wig, the one I kept in my traveling bag, I drove to the nearest storage facility and stashed the painting. This precaution took about an hour to perform. The whole time I worried about my uncle's predicament, but if it came to a situation where I was forced against my will to unlock the storage unit, video camera recordings would complicate matters for my no-good partners. Always have a backup plan, Victor was fond of saying to me.

In the meantime, I called Roman's investigator friend and part-time lawyer and left a message. Where was my dear uncle?

When the phone rang, it was Sadye. "Clara, I'm scared. I tried to call Roman and he doesn't answer. He told me to call him every thirty minutes this evening, and if he didn't answer to call you. What's going on?"

Her concerned tone and my gut convinced me to ask for help. "It's complicated. I need a place to stay for a few hours...until Roman arrives. I know it's close to midnight, but can I wait at your house?" Someone, probably Arthur, was trying to reach me on the burner phone that was given to me for the job. It kept ringing in the background. I wondered if the burner phone was bugged.

Sadye said, "Sure. But —"

"I'm driving to you, to Cabbagetown. Explain everything later." After assuring myself my private cell was charged, I silenced the burner by ripping out the battery and throwing it out the car window.

★ ★ ★ ★ ★

I recalled sort of where Sadye lived on Wylie Street, but it was dark, and I couldn't see the house numbers. By using a local barbershop on the corner as a landmark, then spotting the old woman's Chevette, I found the right residence. The eyes of a cat shone in the headlight beams with an extraterrestrial eeriness as it scurried across the lawn. The front door was open, and as I parked I could see Sadye rummaging through the hallway closet. As usual, she was dressed in a drab skirt and blouse with her salt-and-pepper hair pulled back at the nape of her neck.

Navigating the steps, I peered through the screen door and thought I observed Sadye stick a gun in her handbag. "Knock, knock," I said as Sadye whirled around. "I didn't mean to startle you. May I come in?"

"Yes. Tell me Roman's not in any danger."

"Let's sit so I can clarify the situation." I tried to sound calm. "First, it isn't dire. Roman is fine and will be along soon. We discussed this possibility and how to handle it. In the event that —"

"That what?"

I inhaled, smelling the distracting odor of collard greens. "If one of us got caught —"

"By the polices?"

I shrugged, ignoring Sadye's street pronunciation for police. "Maybe."

Sadye put a hand on her heart. "You tell me, right now, where my Roman is."

"I don't know his exact location, but I called our lawyer."

Sadye dropped her purse on a chair. "Hell, gal, how bad is it?"

Startled by the fact Sadye used profanity, I took a moment to reshape the truth. "Roman and I run a lucrative business together that involves transferring commodities from one place to another for a fee. It can be dangerous."

"You con folks," Sadye said.

I felt myself blink.

"Don't look so surprised. Roman already told me as much. By the way, I'm not the old fool you think I am, and I'm not deaf. The little conversation with Felipe at Hernando's house." Before I could deny it, Sadye continued, "I ran a shot house for years in San Francisco. Ran a lucrative business of illegal gambling and booze out of my house back in the day. Early on, pegged you as the traveling kind. Now, what are you messed up in?"

"We lifted a valuable painting from a local gallery during an event and left our double-dealing partners to fend for themselves, but security caught Roman. So I'm not sure if the locals or Feds have him."

"Or your conniving partners have him."

"Right."

"Okay," Sadye said. "Follow me into the kitchen. I got to turn off the collards." Spooning the greens into a glass bowl, she added, "I have a brother-in-law, a deputy sheriff. He works at the courthouse and can find out if Roman has been arrested. Before I do, I need to know the location of the job and where the painting is now."

"You understand that anything I say about the painting can't be passed on to law enforcement, or Roman and I go to prison for a very long time?"

"I got it, young thang," Sadye said. She shoved the bowl of greens inside the refrigerator and shut the door.

We sized each other up.

Sadye pursed her lips. "Let me guess. You have the painting squirreled somewhere safe with your soft white hands all clean while Roman bites the big one somewhere not so nice."

The remark hit a nerve because I did feel guilty for leaving Roman behind at the MARTA turnstiles. "Look, Lady Sadye, I never liked you, and there's no reason —"

"Just tell me when and where they took Roman down. What county?" Sadye opened a drawer and pulled out her reading glasses, a pen, and a pad. "I need a list of all the players involved so I can call reinforcements, and then later, you and I can compete for Miss Congeniality."

Assessing my limited options, I focused on the rough hardwood floor and paced. I had to admit the old woman had gumption. When I looked up, Sadye was seated in a cane chair filing her nails.

The unruffled matron said, "Hon, you need to trust somebody, and what better person than me? I care for your uncle, and know my way around the system. Trust me. I can help you."

The vintage green-leaf wallpaper pattern in Sadye's kitchen made me recall my mother's kitchen in Dune Park, Indiana. I closed my eyes and inhaled. The combination of spices and scents was different than I remembered, but the underlying sense of safety hung in the air. I took another deep breath looking out the window and my anxiety subsided. I was headed down a path with a woman Roman vetted already. I believed Sadye cared for

Roman. I needed an ally, and I decided to risk it all on my instinct. "Okay, here is what we're up against…"

Sadye lowered her phone. "My nephew told me that Roman isn't registered in the APD Hilton, or any other jail in the area. No John Doe fitting Roman's description in the hospitals either. You're lucky I have my own underground pipeline, including janitors and kitchen staff, because the Feds don't share info easily. I'll hear something in a few hours from my FBI contact." Sadye laughed and pointed a finger at me. "You should see your face."

"I must admit I'm amazed. I underestimated you. You seem…"

"Like a simple maid."

I looked away.

"I'm street smart, not educated by some standards. People see what they want to see. Right, Clara?"

"God, I never meant… I'm sorry."

Sadye patted my hand. "No need for all that. Let's get back to Roman."

I twisted my hair in a bun at the nape of my neck. Besides being embarrassed, something needled at me. "If the Feds don't have him, we must assume Arthur and Felipe are holding him. But where?" I remembered what was bothering me. "Wait a minute. You told me your brother-in-law, not nephew, worked in law enforcement."

Sadye shrugged. "I have many relatives and friends. Does it matter?"

We eyeballed each other. "Bottom line, I don't trust you completely, and I'm not sure you're good for Roman," I said.

"No problem. The feeling's mutual."

Despite myself I smiled. "Fair enough. Temporary truce?"

Sadye nodded.

"I don't want to wait for your Fed informant. I think we should check the basement of the gallery and surrounding warehouses."

"Agreed." Sadye watched me pace.

"Places that wouldn't create suspicion or alert authorities. Arthur owns a warehouse a few blocks from the museum where we practiced the con. Are you in?"

"Yes. That sounds like my son's car pulling up in the driveway now," Sadye said. "He's going with us. We'll need some muscle."

15

Ossie drove up in a glossy white Escalade with dark-tinted windows and waved to Sadye and me on the porch. Roman had forgot to put my jeans in my traveling bag. I retied a pair of LaShaska's baggy sweat pants she kept at her mom's place. I pulled up the elastic-bound hems to my knees and doubled the pant legs back down to my tennis shoes.

"Wow, nice SUV," I said. Before I could stop myself, Sadye caught me looking at her Chevette in the driveway.

Sadye raised her eyebrows. "Oh, you think my son gonna drive a heap like my Chevette. Ossie *owns* a barbershop, and he's a computer whiz. He can afford a nice ride." She gave me a sideways grin. "I can too, but my Chevrolet has sentimental value. Ossie's dad was the love of my life, and he gave that car to me."

A car door slammed shut somewhere on the street. "I never said…"

"You didn't have to. I live where I want and with the peoples and things I want around me. Money ain't got nothing to do with it."

"Lesson learned. You certainly conned me from the start."

"Yeah, nothing better than fooling a white princess."

"I take exception —"

A huge shadow dimmed the illumination from the porch light; I turned and looked up. Sadye's son smiled down at me. How had this linebacker-sized man stepped on the porch without making a sound?

"Ossie, you remember Clara from the picnic?" Sadye said.

"I sure do. Miss Thang and Hernando." He swept his rock-solid arm toward the Cadillac. "Let's go, ladies. I have a lead from my street peeps on where they moved Roman."

It seemed like the night would never end. "What time is it? My cell is dead. Do you have a USB portal?" Nobody bothered to answer me. I scooted forward in the backseat behind Ossie. He was driving and Sadye occupied the Escalade's front leather passenger seat, texting and receiving multiple dings in response.

"You're right, Ossie. The Feds don't have Roman," she said.

Ossie took a gulp of coffee from a QT mug about the size of a six-cup thermos and pointed at the dashboard. "It's 2:55 a.m.," he said, talking over Marvin Gaye's *What's Going On*.

I noticed Ossie had played R&B oldies since we got in the Escalade, and he had used a matter-of-fact, precise tone when it came to numbers. "Right," I said. "Where are we going?"

"Meeting up with some homeboys for backup — they owe me — before we spread a little love to the folks holding Roman…in an abandoned building, the old M Gallery."

I felt a wave of panic. "Sorry. My brain is in second gear. Where?"

"Downtown, sketchy neighborhood."

"That doesn't sound right. Arthur has manicured fingernails."

Ossie shrugged. "Probably chilling in his hotel room. Felipe's the main player tonight."

Sadye received a text message and turned toward me. "It's been verified. Suzanne and Felipe laid low for a few hours in the basement at the gala, but about midnight they and another thug stuffed Roman inside a work van they borrowed from my cuz. Emmett runs a janitorial service at night and saw it all go down from windows on the third floor above the loading dock."

Ossie shook his head. "I told you, Mom. Anyway, they paid him a hundred upfront, then called him a few minutes ago and told him his van was sitting in front of M Gallery with a homeless brother guarding it."

"Sadye, you weren't kidding about contacts. But how do you know which building?"

"The homeless guy and Emmett." Sadye tied her gray hair into a bun. "Turns out you can reach the roof of the building we want from the parking deck next door. Turn in here, Ossie." She pointed across Ossie to an apartment complex entrance off Glenwood Road that led to a rundown red-brick apartment complex, Glenwood Heights.

"Yes, Mom. I got it."

I held onto the handle grip above my window and searched for a persona to fit this situation to quiet my fears. A chain-linked fence divided the long driveway from the apartments next door, and a weed-enhanced dirt lawn the size of a football field separated the three-storied apartments from the road. A fortress.

Ossie pressed a button on the steering wheel column, and Al Green's smooth voice in *Everything's Gonna Be Alright* faded to a low vibration as we neared the top of the hill.

"Second row on the right. Go past the torched building," she said.

"Another cousin?" I laughed. They didn't. Sadye and Ossie exchanged a glance.

"Something like that," he said.

Ossie's headlights lit up the burnt-out apartment building and two young African-American males in baggy clothes. They sat on a weathered couch smoking and drinking from bottles hidden in paper bags. I'd been caught and charged, once upon a time, for open container in Dune Park by the local PD.

Ossie slowed the Escalade and rolled down his window. "Yo, need to speak with JJ. Private business. He knows I was heading his way."

One of the young men stood, pulled his pants up, and ambled over to the car with one hand cupped at his waist. "He's strapped," Ossie said. He leaned back on the console and let the teenager stick his head inside the window and take inventory. The smell of beer and weed filled the space. "You must be good friends of Mr. Z bringing two womens to my turf at night. Not into gray hair, but this white one's nice." He nodded and, showing several gold teeth, grinned.

Sadye snapped her fingers. "Over here, young dog. I'm Z's auntie, young man, and we're in a hurry."

His head jerked back and moved like a bobblehead toy. He stepped away and dropped his hands at his sides. "Wasn't meaning no disrespect, ma'am." He pointed. "Mr. Z in that building, number seven."

The metallic number seven hung loose and upside down on the apartment door. The place appeared uninhabited until you reached the back bedroom. The layout of the room could've been a lawyer's office. Two vintage leather chairs with studs faced the padded high-back office chair behind the library table desk. Break-down-easy shelves and color–coded boxes of files lined the walls. I heard the toilet flush, then a stunning man walked into the room. Wearing slacks and a '70s Italian Gambino shirt, this Zulu-warrior lookalike shook Ossie's extended hand in a series of complicated gestures and hugged his aunt.

They ignored me. It was okay by me.

"Been a long time, Auntie. Good to see you. Please sit." I remained standing while Ossie and Sadye sat across from Mr. Z. "Sorry you had to make a trip down here, but I won't be back in my regular office for a couple of days. You called my emergency number? Right?"

"My man, Clara's uncle," she pointed to me, "is in trouble. They were double-crossed during an art heist and decided to take the painting and run. Clara got away. Roman didn't. The others, the so-called art dealer, his assistant, may or may not be involved, but a hothead Spanish dude named Felipe wants to exchange Roman for the painting. Roman wasn't looking so good when Emmett saw him being carried out to his van. After they left, cuz cleaned up a lot of blood in the basement."

I felt nauseated.

"Is Emmett still working for The Upton or the High Museum?"

"In this case Upton's. But we're headed downtown to get Roman at the M Gallery."

"How many guys you need?" Mr. Z asked, then held up an index finger. "Excuse me for a second."

He turned his electric green eyes on me. "Clara, do you intend to keep the painting or give it up?"

I flinched as I felt a bolt of current between us. "Roman is the priority. He might not see it that way, but it sounds like he isn't in any shape to argue, or make a move."

He returned his focus to Ossie and Sadye. "Will four guys be enough?"

Ossie said, "Yes, I don't expect much firepower, but the Spanish guy offends easily. Wants to be a badass. Mom tried talking to him."

Sadye sat back in her chair. "Something is eating at him besides the painting."

I shifted my stance and cleared my dry throat. They looked at me.

"At our first meet-up about the heist, he followed me into the women's bathroom and tried...anyway, I kicked him in the balls."

Sadye grunted. "And you're dating his brother."

"Yeah, there is that," I said.

"The brother, Hernando, is their forger. Master works of art," Sadye said.

Mr. Z doodled on a pad. "The real and the fake paintings were switched during the heist?"

"Yes," I said, "during a fundraising event."

"Interesting." Mr. Z scanned me, taking stock. "Jealousy is a mean beast." His attention swung back to his relatives. "Okay. Four of my best. Relax for a few minutes. They're close by handling another matter."

A few hours later we were still waiting for Mr. Z's crew to show, but used the time to pick up the Hopper from the storage unit in Chamblee and return to the Southside.

Ossie drove the Escalade into a convenience store at Glenwood and Line Street and stopped at the gas pumps. While he filled the tank, Sadye went inside the store. From the backseat I watched as the sunrise halo backlit a billboard sign displaying a huge Red Bull can. I took a couple of deep breaths and fiddled with the tube containing the original *Girl at Sewing Machine*. I felt invested like the painting was my first puppy, not a masterwork by Edward Hopper.

Waiting for Sadye to return, Ossie pulled off to the side of the building and sang backup to Aretha Franklin's *Respect* playing through his high-grade sound system.

"My mentor taught me about music, from ragtime to the classics," I said. "We're about the same age. How come you like R&B?"

He turned around and stared like it was none of my business. "Yeah," he said, and then he laughed. "I'm messing with you, Miss Thang. You did good back there. You kept your game face on. Kept a low profile. I could tell Z thought you were all right." He paused. "You scared?"

"A little, but I'm more afraid for Roman. How much longer?"

He nodded. "You shoulda had the painting with you from jump street. Wasted our time with a trip to Chamblee." He leaned his elbow on the console. "It's gonna take Z's boys a minute. They taking care of some more business, but they'll show soon, ready to go." He looked at me through the rearview mirror. "Good you're scared. Adrenaline helps you survive."

He stared. I wondered if Ossie was reliving a combat or street shootout experience, but I sensed broaching the subject wouldn't be appreciated. "Is Emmett still downtown? Keeping watch?"

"No, too dangerous. But don't worry. Before he left we made other arrangements."

"I don't understand —"

Ossie held up a palm. "Later."

Sadye opened the car door and handed out coffee and homemade fried pork chops on biscuits, some enterprising Southside mother's money-making project. Delicious. Sadye's phone pinged, and she started texting.

Ossie distributed hot sauce and other condiments as he cut his eyes at me with a sideways grin.

With my mouth full, my sandwich half gone, I stopped chewing. "What?" I said.

"Nothing. Eat up, Miss Thang, you're gonna need it."

Four solemn teenagers armed with Mac-10s, Mr. Z's guys, followed the Escalade in a black Hummer. Under my breath I recited what I could remember of the Roma's version of The Lord's Prayer asking for protection for everyone involved in my uncle's rescue. My ill feelings cast aside, I felt thankful as I called upon the strength of my mother and Aunt Amorosa to bolster me.

I drank in the low ebb of the downtown traffic at 5:30 a.m. A solitary pedestrian here and there, and a couple of cabbies talking and drinking coffee outside a Dunkin' made slow, deliberate movements and informed the concrete city to wake up. I thought of Roman rousting me most mornings with his own signature greeting. "Clear sleep from your eyes, *moya lyubov*. Get up." I missed him. I turned to see if the black Hummer was still behind us.

Ossie used one hand to rotate the steering wheel, circled to the top deck, and parked near the chain roping off M's roof and its back entrance.

A white kid with peach fuzz on his chin came out of the shadows.

Ossie checked his 9mm magazine and chambered a round as the kid unhooked the chain and waved the all clear. Ossie nodded back at the kid, and then caught my eye in the rearview. "Clara, it would be better if you stayed here."

"No. You will need me." I raised the cylinder.

Ossie looked at his mom.

"She's right," Sadye said. "Felipe wants to settle the score with her. A man with a grudge can be distracted."

On the rooftop Sadye opened the cylinder of her .38 and clicked it shut as Ossie stepped back to kick in the door to the studio, but I intervened by blocking the door and producing my utility knife with its handy-dandy tool set from my windbreaker pocket. "No noise," I said.

Ossie stuck a thigh-sized forearm across my chest, and I expected him to push me back, but Sadye said, "Let her be."

Ossie grunted and stepped behind me. Hovering.

The white kid said, "I know a way in."

Before he could race over and steal my thunder, I picked the lock on the door leading from the roof to the inside staircase and returned my knife into my pocket. I could smell the roof tar baking in the morning sun as Mr. Z's gang got out of the Hummer and joined us with their Mac-10s held at their sides.

The white kid, wearing dark jeans and a hoodie, his dark eyes wide open, stood close to Ossie. "Jeremy, you watch and text Miss Sadye if you see PD, or anything else we need to know. If you hear gunfire, don't be peepin'."

"No prob, Boss." Jeremy's eyes never left the Mac-10s.

"If we don't come out in ten, you call The Man yourself, 911 on the burner, and get gone."

"Got it."

Ossie handed him a folded hundred.

"Time to gitterdun, hey, Clara?" He chuckled at his Cracker slang. "Stay between Mom and me."

"Dudes, turn off your phones," Ossie ordered. Everyone complied except Sadye. Her flashlight app remained lit on her phone. Even with the light we felt our way down the steep, narrow stairs. Trailing beside Sadye, I shifted the cylinder from one hand to another as the door shut. The armed teenagers seemed to breathe together creating a push-pull airwave against my backside. Metal touched my arm and I jerked away. I dropped the painting. "Stop," I said without muffling my volume.

Sadye turned, her face an eerie green in the cell's light.

I pointed down and whispered, "The painting."

Ossie scooped up the cylinder near his Air Jordan Retros and tucked the tube under his massive arm.

We wove our way through a hallway, passed an office and restroom, and came to a T-intersection spilling into the M Gallery space. A wall mural and hardwood floors flashed into view as Sadye's light traveled around the room and settled on Roman in a heap on the floor. Close by, Felipe leaned against a crate smoking a cigar. The sight of Roman, bound and gagged, lying motionless on the floor, made my stomach lurch.

"Where is the painting?" Felipe's gaze pierced the shadows and glared at me.

I stepped forward and pulled the painting through the crook of Ossie's elbow, keeping away from his 9mm that was double-gripped and pointing at Felipe.

"I need proof of life," I said.

"Send one of your goons over to check him." An armed teenager behind Ossie began to move around him. Ossie stuck out a hand. "Wait." He looked at Felipe. "Where's your backup? I know you didn't come here alone. Unarmed."

The lights switched on. Suzanne, holding some kind of remote device, flanked us on the right and a Hispanic man, older than Felipe with colder eyes, pointed a semi-automatic at us on our left. For some unknown reason he shot first and the lights went out.

Another shot rang out. I hit the floor. I felt the tube containing the master painting roll away into the darkness. I crawled toward Roman. Adrenaline pumping, for several seconds I swear I could see in the dark.

Grunts, scuffling, and flesh being pounded kept everyone else busy until Sadye screamed. "Find the lights, Big Dewayne. Ossie is bleeding."

The lights popped back on as we heard sirens in the distance. The painting, Felipe, and his crew were gone.

I held Roman's limp hands bound with duct tape, and Sadye cradled Ossie in her arms across the room. She and I nodded at each other. Both men were down but breathing.

I checked Roman for wounds beyond the obvious. He moaned, but never opened his eyes.

Sadye yanked off her blue neck scarf and made a tourniquet. She folded it lengthwise, wrapped it around Ossie's bicep, threaded the ends through the loop, pulled hard, and double-knotted the ties.

"Let's get out of here," Sadye said. "Dewayne, you go with Clara." She threw a set of car keys to him. "Take Roman in the Escalade. Clara knows the way to my house. The rest of you help me get Ossie up. He's going into shock." It took the remaining three guys, their weapons getting in their way, to lift Sadye's son.

I walked around Ossie's smeared blood on the blond hardwood floor as if I saw blood every day, and did what I was told to do. I followed Roman, still semi-conscious, being carried like a sack of potatoes draped over Dewayne's massive shoulders. I bent down and retrieved my uncle's dragging feet. With Roman's knees hitting Dewayne's backside, we marched in a freaky column. We left the same way we came in, only with injuries.

Dewayne parked the Escalade behind Sadye's house, and cut the tape from Roman's hands and feet. We waited for Sadye. Roman stirred once in the backseat, but he never woke up. "They must've drugged him," I said. "If Sadye doesn't get here soon, I'm picking the lock." My silent driver pushed back his seat, folded his arms, and nodded off within seconds. I turned around and studied Roman in the backseat. Patting Roman's hefty knee lying next to the console, I checked my cellphone with my other hand. No messages. At eight o'clock in the morning, I couldn't remember what day it was. I touched the calendar menu on the cell. It was May the fifteenth. Long night. Hard to believe the heist had occurred less than twenty-four hours ago.

A lot had happened since yesterday. The one-way streets surrounding the M Gallery had saved us. Two police cars, blue lights and sirens, raced down Pryor Street, a half block south of the parking deck, and turned on Mitchell as we waited, not breathing, at the red light at the corner of Martin Luther King Boulevard and Pryor Street. Apparently, the reported gunfire on Broad Street didn't include vehicle descriptions, but I kept looking over my shoulder for a third police car. The light turned green, and we merged into the downtown morning rush-hour traffic. We managed to catch the lights just right, turned onto Memorial Drive, through Cabbagetown, and pointed the Hummer toward I-20.

A knock on the Escalade's window made me whip my head around, and my forehead hit the doorframe. It was Hernando. He grimaced an apology as I rolled down the window. In one swift motion my young bodyguard moved across me and stuck a gun in Hernando's face.

"Whooah. I know him," I said, smelling sweat and gun oil emitting from my over-eager friend, the side of his 9mm inches away from my nose.

Dewayne said, "Back away, dude."

Hernando complied with his hands in the air, and we got out of the SUV on the passenger side.

"Turn around." Again, Hernando did as he was told. His Polo shirt and jeans revealing nothing except a trim muscular body.

"This is crazy. Hernando is my…He is Felipe's…Sadye and I know him."

Skeptical, Dewayne said, "Yeah."

I looked at Hernando. "How did you know where to find me?"

"Sadye called. The news is reporting the footage from the street surveillance cameras near the M Gallery will be available soon. May I lower my hands?" Hernando asked.

Dewayne dropped his weapon. "There's stolen plates on both SUVs."

We stared at each other while the information sank in.

Hernando nodded toward the storage shed in the backyard. "She keeps a spare key near the shed underneath an overturned flowerpot. A pink one. And Sadye took Ossie to a pharmacist friend with some medical training to clean and bandage the arm. A clean shot through and through."

Roman moaned.

Hernando tried to peek inside the Escalade. "Is Roman okay? Sadye sounded concerned on the phone."

"I think so, but we need to get him inside. Dewayne, would you get the key?"

He hesitated, but turned and left us.

I got out of the car and hugged Hernando, and he kissed me.

He held me an arm's length away and looked me up and down. "I was so worried. Are you all right?"

"Yes. I'm glad Sadye trusted you and called...under the circumstances."

Hernando flashed his pearly whites at me and shrugged.

Dewayne reappeared swinging a purple key chain, grinning like the kid he was.

I said, "Now you guys decide to smile?" I opened the SUV's back door. "Let's move Roman before a nosy neighbor calls the police."

Dewayne didn't want any help. He cradled Roman in his arms and walked into the shotgun house, through the kitchen, and down the hall to a bedroom. My uncle looked like a vulnerable hibernating bear lying on a twin bed with a floral bedspread hemmed in a double row of ruffles. I smoothed the hair off his forehead and turned to Hernando. "Will you undress Roman? Because of the Roma rules of conduct he wouldn't want me to touch his lower body. Take his shoes off last or wash your hands afterward."

"Of course, whatever you need."

"Please tell me if you think anything is broken."

He nodded.

I went back to the kitchen and paced. I couldn't remember anytime with Victor when our trio had been seriously injured during a con. It was Roman's job to protect Victor and me. I knew nothing about nursing.

I heard a car pull into the driveway and peeked through the vintage seersucker, ruffled-edged curtains. It wasn't the Hummer. Mr. Z stepped out of a gold Cadillac sedan from the passenger side, leaving his driver in the car. As I opened the side door to the kitchen, Mr. Z ducked his head and sauntered through the doorway carrying a duffle bag.

"We meet again," he said, nodding. "How is Roman?"

"I don't know."

He stood close, and I craned back my neck to see more than his chest.

"He was beat up and probably drugged," I said.

"I brought some medical supplies." He lifted the duffle bag. "I learned a few tricks from a medic in Iraq. Helped him get the pain meds he needed for the wounded."

He touched my elbow. A quick jolt of sexual current ran through me. Tears welled in my eyes, and I looked away feeling disloyal to Hernando and, for some unexplainable reason, to Roman.

"Where is Dewayne? I have a job for him." Mr. Z scanned the room.

"In the bedroom on the right with Roman and Hernando, my friend, our friend. Sadye called him."

Mr. Z studied me. I could tell he knew Hernando was more than a friend. He glanced again around the tidy old-fashioned kitchen with a white stove and cabinets. "Boil some water in case I need to sterilize anything, and make us some strong coffee. Everything is going to be all right." Revealing dimples, he smiled and walked down the hallway, leaving a faint scent of pipe tobacco in his wake.

He smelled like Victor, like sanctuary. I warned myself to stay away from this man.

* * * * *

Late in the morning, Sadye and Mr. Z spoke in whispers in the dark hallway. I turned down the news on the television and headed their way, but he kissed her cheek and passed by me in a hurry on his way out without saying a word.

"What is going on?" I asked Sadye.

"He has other business. But he and Dewayne will be back in a couple of hours with some chicken. In the meantime there's collards and some mac and cheese in the fridge."

"Okay, maybe later." My mouth watered. I hadn't eaten since the pork biscuit at the convenience store last night. "How is Ossie?"

"Ossie's gonna be fine. He's at his baby momma's place. She'll take care of him."

We entered the bedroom together to check on Roman. He was hooked to an I.V. bag, but sitting up on the side of the bed, wrapped toga-style in a sheet.

"Roman, get back in—"

Roman coughed and grabbed at his ribs. He grimaced in pain. "Dewayne showed me my face on TV. I am wanted man." He straightened up. "Big trouble."

18

I sat next to Roman tucked into the covers of the twin bed. While he slept, I reread a letter from my mother dated two years ago, but written in Aunt Amorosa's handwriting. The letter read:

> You are now twenty-five years old. How I miss you. Your aunt sees a future without Victor, but Roman will be there always. Do not fret about the things you cannot change. May Saint Christopher protect you, and the Holy Virgin Mother guide you as you become a complete woman. I love you beyond measure,
>
> Your Loving Mother

Roman stirred and opened his eyes.

"I got to say," I winked, "the floral bedspread doesn't do a thing for your complexion." I folded the letter and put it in my oversized robe pocket, another loaner from Sadye.

"You funny, Tinkerbelle, but we need to talk while Sadye is gone."

"You're right. We've sold almost everything we can. The cash we have on hand won't buy fake passports."

"No. I go alone."

"Don't be absurd. You're hurt and will need my help. Besides, we're a team."

"You come later. Safer if I go alone, or with Sadye —"

"Excuse me?" I felt crushed and fingered the letter inside my pocket.

"She has money and contacts. You know I love you, but they look for me with young woman, not Sadye." He motioned for me to hug him.

We embraced gently. He waited until I said, "Okay, I'm smiling," then he let me go

— completing the almost forgotten ritual, a holdover from my dramatic teenage years.

I sat on the bed beside him. He straightened his bruised, stiff shoulders. "Please forgive. I promised Victor I keep you safe, but the photo on news was me before I came to America. They want me for things I did for Mother Russia. Before I knew Victor. And you."

I stood up quickly. "You were a spy?"

"No. I worked for KGB. Eliminate problems."

I sat back down on the opposite bed. The emotional punch made it hard to breathe. "You were an assassin?"

"Enforcer mostly." He held his hands palm up. "I was stupid, hungry kid when they took me from the streets. Filled head with —"

"They brainwashed you."

"I knew nothing but Mother Russia and hunger. They told me my family in Volga died in fire set by young radicals, haters of German Jews. My family owned bakery."

"I never knew…" The seconds ticked by as Roman let his shocking information sink in. I couldn't imagine Roman as KGB. I tried to convince myself it was all right that my uncle was a killer. "You did what you had to do to survive," I said. "I remember how that felt before I met you and Victor. Desperate."

He nodded. "That's not me anymore. Do you believe me?"

"Yes, to me you're the kindest, dearest…letting yourself be handcuffed and beaten so I could get away."

I stood and walked the length between the beds and back again. "But why now? You've been under the FBI radar for over thirty years." In my mind's eye, Felipe's angry face loomed in front of me. "Felipe. I bet he called the FBI. He must really hate you and me."

"Too bad. The toad and his relative — the one looks like him with gun — drugged me and hogtied me, then he hit me and told me what he tried to do to you in bathroom at the Greek restaurant." He pounded his fist against his palm. "He knows I hurt him if I find him."

For a second, Roman's violent past flashed across his face, and I shivered. I needed distance and walked to the round table near the window and kept rearranging a box of packaged bandages, a roll of tape, and sanitary wipes. I remembered feeling proud as I walked out of the bathroom at the Greek restaurant, and now I didn't know what to think. I turned around to face the man, not the hero I'd conjured but a vulnerable person with secrets — essentially all the family I had left.

"I warned him what would happen if you knew. We're in a mess, aren't we, Uncle? I wish Victor was here."

He sighed as he pulled the top sheet tighter around his exposed shoulder. "Some things we cannot change."

I flinched at the same words I'd just read in my mother's letter. "Was Arthur there when they beat you?"

"No. Da nyet. His son overdosed and he's en route to London."

"He is? Is his son —"

The door opened. "All very interesting, but you must stop stewing and fretting. What's this nonsense about hurting someone? You're not in any shape, my dear," Sadye said, putting a food tray on the side table, and then nodding in my direction. "You, Miss Clara, must leave and let Roman rest."

My mouth opened to protest Sadye's eavesdropping, but she said, "So I was listening through the door waiting for a good time to come in. Sue me."

Felipe hugged his goddaughter and noticed her poise. She smoothed her sundress skirt underneath her as she sat down in a restaurant chair beside him. "The bathroom had mirrored walls with engraved zoo animals on them. I hope a local artist made money," she said with a smile. "If not, dad will scold the restaurant owner."

"I agree. Atlanta has its share of world-class artists. You're growing up, Alexandria. Have you become sixteen overnight?"

"You know I'm only ten." She blushed. "Do you approve of the dress? I want to impress my mentor, Professor Fannin, and her husband, and of course, I want to please you and Papa."

"You are beautiful, and the dress is perfect."

"Thank you, Uncle." Alexandria wobbled in her chair. Her toes brushed the concrete floor.

Felipe hoped she liked the upscale eatery with the clean lines made of steel and glass.

She continued, "Are you and Papa still mad at each other? I hate it when you fight."

"Your father and I disagree about business matters, but never about you and your welfare." Felipe patted her cheek. "There is your father, now."

Hernando walked briskly toward them, dressed in his only suit, and apologized for being late. He took Alexandria's hand. "A friend needed my help, an emergency. Regrettable." He gave Felipe a quick glance. "I will explain later, sweetheart." He kissed her cheek. "Where are Mr. and Mrs. Fannin?"

The waiter filled Hernando's water glass and asked if they were ready to order. "We are waiting for another couple," Hernando said.

"Professor Evelyn Fannin's husband," Alexandria said, "has a different last name. He teaches art history." She picked up her menu and browsed.

"His name is Professor Michael Savage," Felipe said. "They had an obligatory event this morning, but they'll be here soon. I spoke to them at the gala and again yesterday. They confirmed our luncheon. They're so proud of Alexandria's last performances at the gala, and then at the Fox." He smiled at his niece. "Your voice sounded magnificent in the Egyptian Ballroom for the Performing Arts Guild event. You impressed a lot of the right people."

Hernando nodded and fiddled with the knot of his tie. "Thank you for picking up Alexandria and escorting her here."

"Of course. My pleasure."

"I hope they want to help sponsor my little songbird's training and eventually her higher education. The time for the application to study at Julliard is approaching so fast." He turned to his daughter, lips puckered in pride of her. "It was only yesterday you were a baby cooing and —"

"Papa, please. Don't. Besides, I want to go to the Curtis Institute of Music." She took a sip of water. "Look. I see them outside." She pointed toward the solarium windows.

Felipe observed the middle-aged couple, dressed in Emory University academic chic, walking across the front parking lot. The curly-headed woman wore her hair loose with a big scarf from an African country across her shoulders, and the man sported a neatly trimmed beard and a dress shirt buttoned up to the bottom of his thin throat.

Alexandria added, "They told me they had good news, but Papa had to be with me. And I wanted you here too, Uncle. I'm so excited. I feel like I'll throw up."

"Relax, both of you. I've got this one." Felipe sat back in the polished aluminum chair and sipped his wine.

Inside the pawnbroker-slash-photo studio, dim lights left the bouncer-looking man at the counter in shadows. Sadye took the lead. "Doug, I want you to meet Clara. She and her uncle need new IDs and passports."

Doug bolted the front door, and then drew a blackout curtain across the window. He flipped on the overhead lights, then walked around the counter as he raised a white forefinger with five dots between his forefinger and his thumb. "Ossie told me to expect you. How soon do you need them?"

"As soon as possible," I said.

Sadye frowned at me. "Roman, my man, needs his ASAP, but Clara's isn't as urgent. You can have a couple more days on hers."

"Good. A new identity with the trimmings takes computer skills and a few days of research. Not like the movies." He rubbed the top of his shaved head.

I noticed a crude prison tattoo of a spider web on his elbow.

He added, "But you already know that. Ossie's the best around. Are you sure you want him involved?"

"Yes," Sadye said. "Just take the photos and make the documents. Ossie will handle the rest."

"Might as well take her photo now." He rolled back a folding partition revealing a stool in front of a backdrop. He lugged a camera on a tripod into position and turned on the studio strobes.

"I could do this with my cell, and I will for Roman, but I'm used to my equipment and the lighting setting mimics the poor quality of an official photo to a tee. Have a seat," he said, and then checked his light meter. "Brunettes love the light. By the way, nice wig."

"Thanks," I said.

"Expensive. Parisian? I have a friend in the biz. Can always spot a good one."

We heard a knock on the side door. "I'll get it," Sadye said, and then left the room.

"So where did you buy the wig?" Doug asked.

"I took this Noriko wig as compensation from a Turkish princess for my psychic readings. Before we start, how much for the IDs?"

Doug changed lenses. "Ask Ossie when he gets here." He fiddled with the camera. "What's your natural color?"

I refrained from answering.

Ossie came from behind the backdrop with his mom and Mr. Z. "Doug's not cheap," Ossie said, "but he owes me. So for you, Miss Thang, we'll work out a deal."

Doug forced a half smile.

I didn't think I'd see Mr. Z again. As the trio approached me, I caught myself buttoning the top button of my V-neck blouse.

Felipe excused himself and followed Professor Michael Savage to the lobby. He left Professor Fannin chatting with Hernando and Alexandria over dessert. Michael frowned as Felipe approached. "For God's sake, man, not here. Leave me in peace to go to the bathroom."

Felipe lodged two fingers on the pressure point located in the hollow of the professor's clavicle. Michael grimaced in pain. Felipe patted his reluctant client's back. "Of course, meet me outside when you're finished. The other interested party has made an attractive offer. If you wish to remain in the running, you should counterbid soon. By the way, I do feel sympathy for your wife. I doubt she knows about your other family. Your other children."

The professor's horse-shaped face turned ashen. "You devil," he said, dislodging his arm from Felipe's grasp. "You're reprehensible. Extortion isn't necessary." His eyes darted over the other people walking through the lobby. He whispered, "I assure you I want the Hopper."

Felipe let him go.

He smoothed his dress shirt. "I will pay your inflated price. The funds for the purchase are in several offshore accounts. It will take a few days but at the very least, you should allow me to verify the authenticity of the painting."

Felipe stepped in front of the professor and blocked his way.

Savage's eye twitched. "There are security procedures in place. I can't obtain the money any faster."

"Go relieve yourself. Afterward, meet me outside near the global village sculpture on the patio."

The professor almost got away when Felipe stopped him and leaned in close to the prof's ear. "Hurry up, Michael, before I lose my patience and change my mind. I could take your money for my silence and sell the painting to another upstanding patron of the arts."

Blinking back tears, I sat in the bedroom chair in Sadye's house and stared out the window. "Where will you go?"

Roman scooted up in the bed. "I decide Croatia. Get lost in islands off her coast. When you come, be easy to travel to other countries."

I gave him a warning look. "You mean Spain?"

"In case you and Hernando want to meet in his homeland." He let me think about the news for a minute. "Since I Russian, I pick up the language quick as jiffy. But Dewayne says most people speak English, and I speak good American English." He grinned.

"Enough to get yourself in trouble. I'm not sure they like Russians or Black folks in

Croatia any more than they do here in the States."

He tried to shrug, but instead grabbed his ribs and groaned. "Sadye will be lioness. I can be Ukrainian, not Russian. Maybe we take their big-time food cruise around the islands, then take another one until you call for us to meet."

I tried to block the visualization of Roman and Sadye together on a cruise. "Sadye has dropped hints about Croatia, so I did a little research. The beaches in the summer sound first rate, but —"

"But taxes for citizens are high." He gave me a pleading look. "Sadye smart woman about money."

"Of course, Sadye has money to invest." I paced in front of the bed. "I see two problems from the get-go: Croatia isn't a non-extradition country, and if we do this, no cons. You need to lay low and not draw attention to yourself."

"I will if you will. No job without me. Agreed?"

"Hmmm…I might need to handle a little unfinished business here before I fly to Europe. My situation is different from yours."

"I be kept man, but Hernando's broke."

"Not what I meant." I walked toward him and kissed him on both cheeks. "But you can't expect me to live on Sadye's money. I'll figure it out. She's already bought the plane tickets. Right?

"Yes. Sadye woman of action."

I sat on the other bed and wrapped my arms around myself. "When do you go?" I felt the tears well in my eyes.

"Three days."

Hernando made espressos while I, wearing one of his T-shirts and my wrinkled slacks, walked around and around the chopping-block island made from a varnished tree stump. My hangover made it hard to think, but I remembered our first night together started with wine, me blubbering on about Roman leaving, and ended up with us in bed. I couldn't remember if I had specifically mentioned Croatia.

"Clara, please sit down. You're making me nervous."

"Sorry. For crying last night and drinking so much. How much did I tell you? When did we go upstairs?"

He kissed me and nodded toward a stool.

I breathed in his scent and sat down.

"Now, good morning, Clara. Here is your coffee. Sugar?"

"Yes, please." I stirred in the sugar and took a sip. "Mmmm…this espresso is divine. Thank you."

"I know. It's my gift."

I laughed. "If last night is any indication, you have many gifts."

"And you." He handed me a scone. "To answer your question, we went to bed around midnight, but alas sleep eluded us. Many hours later…" He smiled, showing his perfect teeth. "I dozed, off and on, but I needed to call my supervisor by six this morning to ask for a sick day."

"Gosh, I made you miss work. So, do we have the whole day together?"

"Until Alexandria calls to be picked up from her singing lesson."

"Oh God, was she here last night?"

"No, no. She spent the night at her mentor's house near Emory. They're preparing for a concert and the rehearsal ran late. Professor Fannin took her to school this morning. Three or four times a year this happens where I have a night to myself. Alexandria's schedule is so busy as she prepares for an event and sometimes she requires tutoring to keep her name on the Principal's List at school."

"That's some pressure for a little girl. Of course, at age ten in the Roma world, my parents were preparing me for an arranged marriage."

"She is a young lady in some ways, but not all. My job is to give Alexandria fertile ground to grow and to flourish in the next few years. Such important years."

I realized my notion of Hernando and me running off to Spain together was selfish and unrealistic, but I was past the point of backing away. It didn't take a fortune teller to see heartbreak in my future. I felt attached to this family man with his many responsibilities and roots. The irony wasn't lost on me.

"Considering what we shared last night I feel uncomfortable asking…Did I say where Roman and Sadye are going to hide out? I wasn't —"

"No, just somewhere close to my home country. 'A couple of hours by plane,' you said." He looked at me with those pleading, soft brown eyes. "Somewhere I might see you when I visit Spain." We reached for each other across the butcher block and forgot about breakfast.

Hernando dropped me off at Sadye's house and kissed me a long goodbye in full view of Ossie, who smoked a cigarette on the front porch and nodded as I passed him.

"You look pretty good for someone whose arm was shot two days ago," I said.

He raised his sling. "I hate this thing, but Moms is hard to say no to."

"Yep, I hear you."

Grumbling about trying to quit smoking, he popped a wad of gum in his mouth and followed me inside. "Miss Thang," he said, "I hope you know what you're doing. Or have you forgot Hernando's brother beat up your uncle, and then had him shot? And the ugly hasn't started yet."

I looked over my shoulder at him. "I do. Life is messy. Haven't you noticed?"

"I can't argue with that." He put his free hand in his pocket. "Felipe needs to be dealt with and Mr. Z and me will take care of it, but we wanted to tell you upfront out of respect for you and your uncle." He reset his ballcap to the side. "Felipe should've kept it clean. Now, blood has been spilled, and the painting is gone. Two sucker punches to zero. Not cool."

"What will you do?"

"Not sure, but Mr. Z don't play. He let the painting go once without asking for a cut. He won't a second time."

I lied. "I already have a plan to retrieve the painting. Would fifty percent of the black market value make him feel better?"

"Most likely. What do you have in mind?"

"Let me have the rest of today to do a little more research. I think I know who the potential buyer might be."

"Step ahead of you. Mr. Z had Felipe followed. He's squeezing a professor at Emory. His wife has old money from the plantation days, in offshore banks making it complicated, or the Hopper would be history already."

"Do you intend to rob Felipe, or the professor?"

"Maybe both."

The acidic taste of fear filled my mouth. "When?" I asked.

"I'll get back with you on that."

Felipe sat at his usual table with a booth bench on one side. While his laptop was updating his security, he drank coffee and gazed around the room. The bagel and soup restaurant was empty except for the big guy with prison tattoos on his fingers working the keys in overdrive on the other side of the room near the cash register. The tattoos had caught Felipe's attention when he had purchased his dark roasted. The zero-sized Asian waitress brought the bald man another Danish, like he was a regular customer, and gave him an over-the-shoulder smile as she walked away with her dollar tip. For a moment, Felipe felt something close to jealousy, then the thrill of the chase kicked in. He'd waited long enough. He bet himself he could fuck the Asian doll without wasting a dollar on her. He flipped his computer closed and tucked it under his armpit as he walked up to the cash register and motioned for the waitress to lean across the counter. Felipe could see down her blouse when she propped her hands on the counter and stuck her chin forward. The tops of her grapefruit-sized breasts were cupped in a lacy purple bra. He whispered in her ear, "You're gorgeous, and I'm rock hard, right now."

She drew back and pretended to be surprised, but she looked him up and down, cocked her head, and then settled on the diamond pinkie ring on his left hand. She smiled and nodded toward the rear of the store as she unbolted the slide lock to the employee gate, and Felipe pushed it open with a knee and followed her.

Felipe smiled. This wouldn't take long.

Doug waited a couple of minutes and followed them to the back.

★ ★ ★ ★ ★

At Sadye's place the next day, I followed Ossie to the backyard near the shed. Dark clouds hung low in the sky, and I heard a dog barking down the street.

Making sure we were alone, Ossie scanned the adjoining neighbors' yards. "Mr. Z wants half the money from the sale of the fake…and the original painting," he said without compunction.

I took a step back. "I guess I don't have any choice. I need money to leave the States."

"Good enough," he said. We shook hands, but I regretted it immediately.

He continued. "Felipe and the professor dude will meet up on Friday night at a big public shindig." Ossie shrugged. "The professor's idea. He is scared shitless."

"Roman will be gone by then. That's good, but how do you know this info?"

"My woman bumped up against him, took his phone, and returned it later while the man was in some fancy restaurant with his wife, Felipe, Alexandria, and Hernando."

"What?" I was alarmed he knew Alexandria and Hernando by sight.

"She lifted his cell. *Bugged* it? Duh." Ossie shook his head. "I already hacked into Felipe's laptop, so after the meet, I'll transfer Felipe's take, maybe a little more, into Mr. Z's account."

"How? When? What about Arthur? Isn't the money routed through him?" I felt the first raindrops on my face.

"Not with this double-dealing piece of shit in charge. Arthur thinks he's in control, but he won't be back from London until a few hours before the meet. It's amazing what people type in their computers at coffee shops." He laughed and pulled up his hoodie over his ballcap. "He has a thing for Asian escorts. No big surprise, but… Anyway, Miss Chu, a waitress with a cute bootie, distracted him in the backroom, while Doug snuck in behind them and copied Felipe's system on a flash drive." Ossie's cell beeped, and he checked it.

"But…"

"He had to put the laptop down to…get down and dirty."

"Yes, I get it. Was the waitress a plant?"

"No. Doug followed Felipe to that soup and bagel place on several occasions, but he didn't go inside." He shrugged. "This time Doug got there first and paid Miss Waitress a little sumpin'-sumpin' extra to flirt and swish." Ossie texted with his thumbs working like biotic appendages. "When it goes down, I need you to bring Hernando to Mr. Z's crib. He'll need to verify the painting is for real. Z's buyer is a guy you don't want to piss off."

"I'll ask, but he probably won't want to get involved."

"So don't ask. He doesn't want Mr. Z and his guys to roll into Reynoldstown and knock on his door."

The rain stopped without warning.

Stone-faced, Ossie stood feet apart and arms folded.

My stomach lurched. "No," I said. "That won't be necessary." Although asking Hernando for this favor would strain our fragile, budding relationship, I knew putting Alexandria in danger would be unforgiveable.

He nodded in the direction of the house. "We better go back inside before Moms chews us out about no common sense...standing in the rain."

"Does Sadye know about the new deal with Mr. Z?"

"Oh, she knows, mostly her idea. But Roman doesn't so keep your mouth shut. Mom's a little busy tying up loose ends before she and Roman leave for Croatia. Mr. Z will give her a call when it's over."

I wondered how far I could trust Mr. Z, if he was a man of his word. I could end up stranded with nothing. Even more unsettling was the agenda Miss Sadye might be hiding. This was the woman Roman would be relying on to help him escape. He could end up in a federal pen.

Roman and I treated ourselves to a steak dinner and registered in what we considered a fancy motel where the sheets and bathrooms were clean and breakfast was included in the room rate. I knew tonight would be our last evening together for a long time. Under the surface I felt a shift in our relationship. During dinner we'd been avoiding talking about him leaving the country with Sadye but me staying put. He hit the elevator button for the third time. He said *blyat*, a word I recognized as a Russian cuss word. "I'll miss you, *moya lyubov*," he said, shaking his upper body like a wet cat. "Doesn't feel right. I cancel trip. Dye my hair blond and wear an earring."

I laughed. "I love you too, but you a blond? No way. I want you to be safe. I will see you in less than a month…unless you're not telling me everything."

"I never lie to you." He looked hurt.

"I didn't mean it that way. When you're in a relationship sometimes…damn it. Maybe Sadye wants, or needs you to keep some things in confidence."

"No. We agree. You are like daughter to me." He held the elevator door for me to exit. "I worry for you alone in big city without me."

We passed by a young couple with a toddler in tow in the hallway.

"I'll be all right. Hernando and I are together a lot —"

"Remember to lift rock to see under. Sex is hot in beginning, but —"

"Roman, don't be crude." I turned to make sure the couple was out of earshot. "We're having a normal adult relationship. It's new and a bit awkward."

He shrugged and swiped the security lock to our room. "Not my business. You grown woman, but the boyfriend's brother is rabid dog. If he bite you, you die."

"I know, Uncle. I have a plan. You must trust me to take care of myself. To use what you and Victor taught me."

Inside the room he put his hands on my shoulders. "I put you in danger if I stay, but you brave woman. Strong." He struck a bodybuilder pose and swished around on his tiptoes. He stopped in front of me and grinned. We played the game we hadn't played since I was in my teens. I tried to push his biceps down, but they were immovable, massive guns. He attempted to give me one of his famous bear hugs, but he groaned and backed away.

"Your ribs. Are you sure you're well enough to ride in a plane for umpteen thousand miles?"

His brow wrinkled. "It's nothing. Little pain keep me…How you say?" He pushed his hands up and widened his eyes.

"Alert?"

"Yes, alert. FBI should bite me."

I laughed and gave him a gentle hug. I thought I saw tears in his eyes when he pulled away, but he said, "Time for vodka," and rummaged in his suitcase until he found the bottle.

"Time to celebrate." He unwrapped two glasses near the ice bucket and poured two double shots of vodka. "To new life in new country," he said with bravado.

We clicked our glasses and drank.

Felipe shielded his eyes from the bright, afternoon sunlight with one hand as he knocked on Hernando's door in Reynoldstown. The new revamped porch smelled like cut wood. He checked the bottom of his Italian loafers and saw sawdust clung to the bottom of his shoes. Disgusted, he wiped his feet on the mat and rang the doorbell. Halfway expecting Alexandria to be home from school and to hear her bouncing down the stairs, he shifted the

Hopper painting in the leather portfolio case from one armpit to another and compartmentalized his wish to see his niece in lieu of the business at hand. He was relieved when only Hernando appeared in the doorway. "Come inside. I was about to have an espresso. Would you like one?"

"Yes, thank you."

His Testoni Moro monk-strap shoes were handcrafted from the finest alligator leather in the whole world. He meticulously wiped down the shiny toes with a silk handkerchief. Why, the pair had cost him thirty-eight thousand dollars US. He placed the encased Hopper on the dining room table, then followed his brother into the kitchen.

Unable to resist, Felipe asked, "Where is Alexandria?"

"She's working on a school project at a friend's house. Here," he said as he used both hands to give Felipe a cup of steaming coffee. "I just made this one." Hernando turned his back and began the process of brewing another.

Felipe leaned against the kitchen counter and sipped a perfect espresso. He studied his brother's profile, the distant look, and the spattered oil colors on his work shirt. "I brought the painting for you to authenticate."

"I gathered," Hernando said. "I'll take it into the studio where the light is better in a minute, but first…"

"You need a break. What've you been painting?"

"I started a new portrait of Alexandria late last night, then put most of the others in chronological order. I think I have more than enough good ones for a small to medium size exhibition space. I picked out twenty-five. The question is do I want to expose her and me to public scrutiny?"

"I see. It's the old dilemma of owning your talent. What would happen if you became successful?" He paused before he added, "What if someone dug deep enough into your past and found out about your prison record?"

"What would Alexandria think?" Hernando said.

"She isn't a baby anymore. She should be told at some point."

"Possibly, but not today." Hernando stirred a teaspoon of sugar in his coffee.

"Invest in yourself. Frame the darn things. My treat. I'll be comfortable after the Hopper is sold. I'll donate to the cause."

"No. You keep your money," Hernando's words spat in his brother's face.

Felipe turned, put his cup in the sink, and rinsed his hands. "You SOB, always so self-righteous."

"Felipe!" Hernando said.

He dried his hands on a paper towel. "Idealism can exist because the realists deal with the shit. It's quite simple. You authenticate the Hopper here, now, and later in the presence of my client, then offensive business of expediting millions of dollars into my bank account will occur. Such a disgusting transaction for an idealist, but you will do it, or little Miss Clara Con might fall down and not get up."

I watched from the hotel main entrance as Sadye and Roman waved goodbye and drove off in a taxi. He was an anxious flyer, and with his injuries the long flight to Croatia would be a challenge. I felt chilled in the frigid air conditioning and poured myself a cup of complimentary coffee from a carafe. Despite the cold lobby, going back to the empty room without Roman felt like a step I wasn't ready to take. Besides, I hoped the maid would discard the drained vodka bottles strewn around the room before I returned. My cottonmouth and aching body indicated my hangover wasn't going away soon. The smell of sausage from the breakfast bar nauseated me. I sat and stared at CNN on the overhead flat-screen television and ignored the white noise from the early risers. Why hadn't I grabbed my sunglasses off the dresser? I caught myself tracing the geometric pattern in the floor tile with a foot when my cell rang. Hernando's number flashed on the screen. I snatched up the phone.

"Hello. Where are you?" he said.

"At the hotel. Sadye and Roman just left. I'm…"

"You must come to my house to celebrate."

"What?"

"I switched the paintings. Felipe brought the Girl to my house to make sure it was the Hopper, but he made a mistake. He threatened to harm you; I slid one of my brilliant replicas of the lovely Girl back into his valise before he left."

"Oh, no."

"You need the money, and Felipe should learn a lesson."

"Okay. Let me think." I stood up and paced around the room trying to block out the noise at the front desk and breakfast buffet. "You must switch them back. What if the buyer brings their own expert?

"According to Felipe the buyer considers himself an expert, an art history professor. He sat on a semi-professional board of examiners." Hernando paused, and it sounded as if he was moving some papers. "He was asked to step down. His pride won't allow him to hire another specialist."

"Still...Felipe will blame you when he finds out the paintings were switched."

"To Hades with my brother," he said. "Forgery is what I do."

"Yes, but —"

"Let me explain. The material dating and forensic investigation can be handled, as you say, by a simple con, a test in the back room. A fake authentication certificate with an accredited board name at the top will be proffered along with a believable provenance, the historical documentation of ownership since 1921. Compared to the old masters, most of Hopper's signatures require only a small amount of research. Easy."

"No. No," I said. "You don't understand." I lowered my voice. "Other people are involved in the purchase of the painting now. Bad people. They want that painting and half the money from the sale of the fake."

"What people?"

I glanced at the clerk, who appeared focused on taking a reservation over the phone. I put another thirty feet between us before I answered Hernando. "Sadye's son, Ossie, and his uncle, Mr. Z — a new character in the saga, a drug lord."

"A drug dealer? How long have you known about these men, their plans, and not told me?"

"Hernando, I care for you, but this is my problem, my business. You have Alexandria to consider." I realized my adamant voice had echoed across the lobby.

The clerk at the registration desk coughed and wrinkled her brow at me. A disheveled father at the check-in desk dropped his credit card on the floor while his twin teenage boys argued about the length of the outside pool.

I turned my back to the clerk and walked outside. The glass doors automatically closed behind me. "Are you still there?"

"Yes. Alexandria is always my first concern," Hernando said in an edgy tone. He paused. "Felipe ordered me to attend the exchange at Barnett Hall on Friday. Did you know?"

"Not the exact location, or your direct involvement," I said, "but I knew Mr. Z wanted you to be escorted to a private viewing, his choosing, after the original was in his possession. I guess he didn't know you'd be at the art center. Anyway, I declined to ask you, but Ossie countered with an unpleasant description of a scenario where Mr. Z's thugs would arrive at your home and do more than insist. I was afraid for Alexandria —"

"You didn't confide in me. You decide for me, my family, what is best? So we are not as close as I thought." He paused. "This makes me very sad."

My head ached. For a moment I closed my eyes against the glare of the morning sunlight and retreated back inside. "Please, Hernando. Roman is gone. The only family I've got left. I may never see him again. I'm...off kilter....Hernando, Hernando?"

But I was speaking into dead air space.

I felt alone.

★ ★ ★ ★ ★

"Excuse me. Professor Savage, you remember the Baroness from the gala," Arthur said.

I stopped at bottom of the stairs and shook hands.

Arthur held his hands out. "She has a stake in the sale of the painting. It's safer for everyone if we stay together until the merchandise is sold."

I felt like a third wheel, but Arthur, and in private Mr. Z, insisted I be at the meeting.

If something went wrong, my instructions were to text Doug, but I figured in the big picture I was the fall guy — or in this case, the fall gal.

I took a deep breath and reconnected with my environment. The Barnett Hall Fine Arts Center, a beautiful old lady with fine wooden bones and a sturdy stone expansive exterior, demanded a certain respect. We climbed the staircase as I wondered how many debutantes and brides had floated down the stairs to start a new phase in their lives. I traced the railing with my fingertips as I kept ascending and closed my eyes. Feminine restriction lay underneath the comfort and security. The price most women paid to maintain their relationships and family traditions was too dear a cost for me.

Hernando had kept his distance since our last conversation about Alexandria's safety. With concentrated steps, my estranged lover pushed against the carpet runner on the stairs and balanced a leather sachet containing the painting and a hard case with equipment for the so-called authentication.

At the top of the stairs Felipe and Arthur guided Professor Savage, Hernando, and me through an atrium with high ceilings, large windows on one side overlooking the gardens and walkways. Classrooms lined the adjacent side of the huge open space that struck me as comforting like a library, but somewhat wasteful.

We passed an empty dance studio, the door ajar, with a ballet barre, but I didn't notice any wall mirrors. We entered an assistant's office with a desk tucked between a radiator, a small window, and a chair. Folders and papers piled high on three corners of the desk forced the young woman to look up from her computer and peer at us over a stack of books on a side chair. She raised eyebrows, fingers suspended above a keyboard, nose ring reflecting fluorescent light, and waited for an explanation for the disturbance.

Arthur withdrew an envelope. "For you, my dear. We won't be long." He nodded toward the interior office door.

She pinned her laptop to her ribs with an elbow, slid around the obstacles on and around the desk, and took the envelope. "Stand still," she said to me. Her spikey black hair tipped with an aquamarine tint didn't move as she grabbed a raggedy backpack from the floor behind my feet. I caught a whiff of cigarette breath as she stood up. She elbowed me as she tucked the laptop and the envelope inside the bag.

"Be gone by the time I get back from my lunch break. My boss doesn't work Fridays. The door is open," she said, then gave each of us a derisive glance reserved no doubt for most of the human race. As she threw the backpack over a shoulder, she grazed Hernando's nose.

I grinned at him and tried to catch his eye. He dropped his gaze.

Inside the interior office, I watched Savage and Hernando, his dark hair flopping over his brow as he stooped over what I hoped was the original Hopper lying on the administrator's leather-topped conference table. The desk, like the room, was small and intimate. Felipe stood with his arms folded close to his computer behind Hernando and Savage. I shifted my stance to lean against the closed door, and Hernando's cold eyes passed by me like I was one of the five chairs in the room. I made myself stand still.

"Baroness, turn off the lights," Hernando said without glancing up.

I did as commanded and moved a bit to the side to get a better view of the table.

Hernando switched on an ultraviolet light to inspect the painting further. "Do you see the brush strokes here, and how Hopper refuses to blend the colors on the canvas?"

"Yes, his illustration training was his curse and his saving grace. One has to eat." Savage put on gloves. "Some critics never considered him a fine artist until after his death, but the driving emotions underneath the realism make the oils and watercolors all the more valuable to me. Impeccable technique."

"I feel," Hernando touched his chest, "as an interloper unwilling to disturb her blissful concentration. The light is so —"

"Delicate, but still American straight-forward simplicity," Savage said, nodding while holding his chin.

I felt confined in the four-foot space left for me to occupy near the corner of the room. I exhaled. "It's glorious," I said. "Can we move this along?"

Arthur shot me a look and stepped forward. He brushed his palms back and forth as his body hovered over the girl in the painting. "Unsophisticated purity certainly has its allure."

I shivered studying Arthur's profile in his expensive suit. He wasn't just a cad. My God, Victor's brother was a perv. As if being controlled by an outside source, I glanced over my shoulder toward the wall behind me, the contiguous wall shared by the room next door. Not smart. Doug was hiding in there, and the others didn't know. Mr. Z had covered his bases. In case something went wrong. "Muscles and brains" would be on site to eliminate problems — including me.

I assumed Doug, Mr. Z's computer whiz, would transfer the extorted sum for the painting to his boss's account the second Felipe left the building with Savage. It didn't matter to me. I was instructed to wait for my cut to be parceled out from Ossie's share. Cash only. With Sadye in Croatia, I wondered if Ossie would keep his word and adhere to honor among thieves.

Savage took an excruciating few minutes to read the documents and held them out. "I realize I don't have a choice," he said, "what I pay for the Hopper, since you interjected extortion, but I do think it's fair I go home with the original."

Felipe grabbed the documents from Savage's hands.

"I don't understand," Hernando said.

"It's quite simple. These papers can't be certified copies made from the originals," Savage said. "Edward Hopper's wife, Josephine Nivine Hopper, kept explicit records. Her style is distinct. These documents are fakes."

Felipe and Hernando said, "No," together. They gave each other a sideways glance.

Arthur cleared his throat. "Josephine and Edward were married in 1924, three years after he painted the girl sewing."

Savage rubbed the furrow between his eyebrows. "Perhaps, you are correct. This situation is tiring, and I wish for it to end."

"Of course," Hernando said. "What other documentation do you require? On top of the extensive provenance, here is a letter from Edward Hopper's favorite, now deceased, aunt. She claimed the painting was in her possession on her bedroom wall while she recuperated from a fall before Josephine gave it to the Thyssen-Bornemisza National Museum in Madrid. As you know, it was and is still — as far as authorities are concerned — on loan in Atlanta for a special showing at The Upton during Museum Days throughout the rest of May."

"Yes, yes," Savage said. He walked over to the Hopper and examined the artist's signature through his LED pocket magnifying loupe one more time. Sweeping his hand in the air above the painting and the documents, he said, "Let's finish this distasteful transaction. I need a drink and the information about my family in Duluth to be protected…to disappear from the web."

Felipe spoke up. "My computer guy is the best at removing online court records etc., and we'll do what we can, but secrets are a thing of the past with social media. Your children have plastered your face in family photos all over Snapchat, etc. With the cloud you can erase data, but bits and pieces remain unless you completely wipe your online presence, and that would send up a red flag. If we can't completely remove it, we can bury it. If family number one finds out about family number two, or vice versa, it won't be from us." Felipe took a step forward into Savage's personal space. "FYI: You might consider putting a new identity in place before you and your penis decide to commit to another family beyond the two you already have."

"You're an asshole," Savage said, but he blinked first and took a step back.

"Maybe, but your first wife better recommend my niece for a full scholarship to Curtis."

"Fuck you."

"Enough," I said. "Give Felipe the codes to your offshore banks and the passwords to your home laptop. Once the money transfer is completed you walk out of here with a masterpiece, and in 24 hours your family secrets are protected. Even the FBI won't be able to trace them without effort."

Savage studied Felipe.

"She's right. If you don't, I'll take matters into my own hands," Felipe said. He turned and walked toward a low bookcase with a computer atop, and opened the computer where the IP address was disguised through a proxy server. "Come here," he ordered over his shoulder to Savage.

Shoulders drooping, Savage followed.

I nodded the all clear to Hernando. Felipe and Savage's attentions were completely focused on the computer — behind us. The mark recited the codes and passwords with a tinge of tenderness like he was telling us his children's names.

I timed the transaction on my cell, as if it would help matters, and watched Hernando slip the original into the middle desk drawer and unroll the fake from a carrying tube. I reset the four mini felt-backed paperweights to the corners.

The money transfer was completed in 35 seconds. Hernando waited for my signal. As Savage and Felipe turned around, Hernando began rolling up the fake painting for the carrying tube.

Realizing I was holding my breath, I exhaled. It was almost over.

Hernando scanned Mr. Z's office wild-eyed and looked at me with suspicion. "Where are we?" he said, smoothing his hair with both hands.

I picked up a drawstring laundry bag from the floor. "I had nothing to do with this," I said as I sat in the other chair in front of the desk. "Because they duct-taped your hands and used this thing to cover your head to bring you here, I guess it's in your best interest for us not to discuss it. Are you okay?"

He rubbed the red rings around his wrists. "Yes, but I have never been treated so…so…"

"Mr. Z and his men will be here in a few," Ossie said, making Hernando whip his head around. He stood behind us by the door, scrolling through his cellphone. The canister with the painting was propped against the wall beside one of Ossie's legs.

I noticed the shelves were empty, and a couple of moving boxes were stacked in the corner. In fact, the place smelled like an old house for sale. Unwanted and abandoned. "Looks like Mr. Z is moving," I said.

"None of your business, Princess. It's best if you keep yourself to yourself." Ossie put his phone in his pants pocket.

"Was all this cloak and dagger stuff necessary? Hernando and I already agreed to come for the authentication."

"I just follow orders. The man has his reasons."

The door opened as Ossie took out his Glock and aimed at a possible threat. The armed teenagers from the M Gallery fiasco, the one who had carried a bleeding Roman into Sadye's house, and Dewayne stepped through the doorway ahead of Mr. Z. Two more teenage bodyguards wearing dark glasses followed. They didn't have visible firepower, but I knew they were carrying at least semi-automatics.

"Relax, bro," Dewayne said to Ossie.

They stared at each other until Mr. Z said, "Clamp it down. We have business." He walked around Dewayne and slid into the chair behind the desk. He smiled and took the time to settle in his chair. "Now, you must be Hernando. I apologize for your rough manner of transport, but it was necessary. My past experience with your brother doesn't help me to trust you."

"I see," Hernando said. "I am not my brother. Would you like me to verify the Hopper now?"

"Yes, we will get to it in a minute. It is a formality." He waved his hand at Ossie to bring the canister to him. "You could lie, but if you do, I will kill you. Then your darling Alexandria will be raised by your brother... or worse."

Hernando's lips thinned, and the color drained from his face. "I wouldn't put my daughter in danger," he said in a calm voice, but I noticed his fist clinched at his side.

"Very good." He turned to me. "Miss Clara, you need to disappear with your new I.D. and passport in hand. ASAP. Do not come back to the States, either with or without Roman. It's laughable the Feds, and by now probably the CIA, think you're communist plants, spies, not just thieves." He opened the canister lid and nodded at Hernando to proceed with the inspection. As Hernando unrolled the painting, Mr. Z moved to the front of the desk and sat on the corner closest to me. He reached for me, his large hands moving down to my wrists. He applied pressure. "Never try to contact me, or anybody connected with me in the States after you go. Understand?"

I swallowed. "Got it."

I changed my clothes in my current motel off I-20 near Moreland to holey jeans, a T-shirt, and inexpensive tennis shoes. Three long days had passed without a word from Ossie. I called him and left another voice mail as I walked east on Glenwood Road outside the Perimeter in the late morning sun. "Look," I said. "We're practically family. You do right by me, and I'll leave and never bother you again." I hung up, hoping the tone of my voice didn't betray how worried I felt. I decided to treat myself to a hearty lunch and found a pub advertising on a sandwich-board sign their daily special of cheese grits and shrimp. On the way back I bought a bottle of vodka at a local liquor store and gave my change to the homeless guy begging outside.

"God bless you, sister. I haven't eaten in a while," the pungent man said as he stuffed the bills in his grimy shirt pocket. He smiled with rotted teeth and hightailed it toward a fast-food burger joint across the I-20 bridge. I didn't need to count the amount of cash I had left. It was less than twenty dollars. The concealed five-hundred-dollar gold necklace around my neck would pawn for about fifty. I hated it, but it was time to call Roman and Sadye and ask for help. Besides my pride, there was another stumbling block: Doug knew how to contact them, but I didn't.

Being cut off from Roman and stranded without funds made me remember my first encounter with Roman and Victor in the train station in Dune Park. I was a hungry ragamuffin. Roman had given me a homemade roast beef sandwich and asked why I ran away. He listened. I learned he was Russian Roma. He understood my background…its traditions and customs. "A wolf will eat a sheep. You should be married to protect your virtue, but your face tells me you're stubborn." He folded his massive arms across his broad chest. "You could travel with Victor and me." He pointed to a man wearing an ascot asleep on a bench.

"No hanky-panky. We give you your privacy." He pursed his lips. "But what do you do?" he said, rolling his hands. "Your Roma talent?"

"I sort of read palms and foretell the future. My mother and aunt have the gift."

"Good." He slapped his knee. "Victor will like that. He played big part in Shakespeare, and famous guy's plays, but sometimes, people want for…entertain at party."

"Entertainment. Right?"

He nodded.

"So I could read palms at parties. What do I get out of it?"

"Fair-square deal."

"A third?" I asked.

"You talk to the boss." He nodded toward Victor. "You can always leave. Up to you." He handed me a ticket to Chicago. "You take my ticket. Cash it in if you want." He patted the bench. "I'll buy another one. Maybe I see you on train." He left an apple on the bench and walked away.

I missed Roman. I opened and shut the motel door. I didn't bother to turn on a light. The darkness soothed me. I flopped on the bed, curled up with my unopened vodka bottle and until I fell asleep hummed Roman's favorite karaoke drinking song, *Take A Chance on Me* by ABBA.

★ ★ ★ ★ ★

The next morning the maid knocked on the door at 11:00 a.m. and reminded me it was checkout time. I brushed the disheveled hair from my face, told her I was staying another night, and shut the door. As I drank the bitter coffee from the one-cup brewing pot, I threw on some clothes and called a car service. I didn't see any reason to call Doug again and give him a heads up. He wasn't going to want to share his information. Ossie and Doug were buddies, and Ossie wouldn't want his mom to know he wasn't playing nice.

Twenty minutes later the cloudy sky spat some raindrops on the windshield of a weather-beaten Volvo sedan as the female driver asked for my destination and drove away, leaving the motel's covered entrance behind. The driver didn't try to make conversation. The reporter on the NPR radio news channel was interviewing a parent about the challenges of raising an autistic child. My problems seemed small in comparison. If Doug refused to help me, I'd think of something.

I hadn't pulled off a con by myself since I was in my pre-teens, but I'd start small and keep my eyes open for the big score, the stake that would fund my trip to Croatia. I knew how to play a part and perfect a costume for the persona out of little to nothing.

"The rain has stopped. You want me to wait for you?" the driver asked.

"Yes, please. Give me five minutes." The driver pulled into the parking lot behind the pawnshop.

When I knocked on the shop door, nobody answered. I went around to the side entrance where Sadye took me the first time to meet Doug for my passport photo. The doorknob turned; I went in unannounced. I couldn't see Doug, but I heard voices in the back room. I shuffled my way through semi-darkness, extending my hands until I reached the passageway leading to his office. I was about to call out when I heard a gunshot, then a series of shots. I ran in the opposite direction.

When I got outside, my ride was gone. The dumpy chicken joint across the street looked like my closest haven. I ducked inside as the bottom fell out of the sky and sheets of rain hit the glass storefront. The cops and EMS arrived right after the rain stopped again and before the grease on my chicken got cold. Fear made me ravenous.

I watched them bring out a Latino man on a stretcher. From this distance I wasn't sure, but he could've been the man who shot Ossie at the M Gallery. The store manager and cashier came out from behind the counter and stared at the three sets of blue lights and two ambulances blocking the right traffic lane across the street. "I heard the gunshots." The cashier scratched her scalp through tight braided hair. "Somebody's dead over there."

"Did you see anybody leave?" asked the middle-aged man wearing a collared shirt with a stiff company logo.

The teenage girl swung her head back and forth making the long braids with clear plastic beads click as they settled around her neck. "I saw a car drive away with a woman in it. An older green four-door, like grandmas drive." She turned toward me.

I kept eating with my head down.

"But she wasn't the shooter. Was sitting in the alley with the engine running the whole time while I was on my smoke break."

"You saw from out back?"

"No. I was watching near the dumpsters on the side."

"Latisha, what I been telling you? You need to smoke behind the restaurant, health inspectors be around and chew my aaa---" he glanced my way "...my behind," he said. "But I guess this time it was a good thing." The apparent manager reset his ballcap.

"Always wondered how that white man kept a pawnshop going. At the end of a hard month, I dropped by for a look-see for a temp pawn, and he tried to lowball me on my wife's engagement ring. Cubic zirconia, my ass."

"Sorry, miss," he said to me.

"No problem," I said.

The manager walked away. "I gotta go do the monthly."

An older white cop, moving slow, strode through the dirt parking lot of the nail shop directly behind the pawnshop and hit a car key remote. A car beeped. He roped off a small area around the car with crime scene tape, and then directed a county van into the alley. A couple of crime scene techs opened the side door of the van and put cloth covers over their shoes and grabbed their cameras. Detectives showed up and peered inside the car and talked to the veteran cop for a two-minute briefing before they walked inside.

I finished my chicken and wiped my hands on several paper towels. "Could I have more sweet tea, please?" I asked the cashier as I moved to the counter.

"Sure." She refilled my glass. "You welcome to stay for the rest of the show, but maybe you don't want to be here when they send police over here to ask questions."

"Right. Thanks. I just wondered if anyone else got hurt. I wasn't —"

"What I don't know isn't a lie." She shrugged. "It will be on the news tonight."

"What is the cross street near the Super Foods on Candler Road."

She told me McAfee Road and used a thumb to point behind her.

"How much for a paper hair cover like your cook is wearing?"

She pulled open a drawer under the counter and handed me a beige cover-up. "You better go on now. They'll be coming out with a body in a bag soon."

I thanked her, looked over my shoulder, and put the cover over my hair. I called a taxi as I cut across the parking lots of two fast-food joints and headed for Super Foods with my iced tea in hand. As I came up to a half-demolished concrete retaining wall, I stopped long enough to tie my black shirt around my waist and expose my white undershirt. All I needed to do was not draw attention to myself, cross Candler Road, and wait for my ride.

I watched a Hispanic mother and toddler cross the street and run for the bus stop in the middle of the block. I followed them. A bus slowed down and stopped on the other side of the street. I felt a car fly past my backside as I cleared the center line. The near-miss changed my mind about the taxi. My luck wouldn't hold out much longer. I ran to catch a ride to anywhere the bus went.

Felipe waited in Arthur's hotel suite for his cousin to call and to say the job was done. He brushed his damp hair back. His early morning swim had cleared his head. He wanted Mr. Z dead and his painting back, but first things first.

Arthur commented on an article in *The New York Times*, but Felipe wasn't listening. He flipped through the channels and found the local news on the television.

Room service knocked on the hotel door, and Arthur wrapped himself in a thick terrycloth robe and went to sign for their meals. He had come through with the information about Doug Dalton. Given the opportunity, the art dealer liked to sneak around and rummage through women's purses and, maybe, confiscate a small memento. On the day they'd met at a coffee shop, and then later at Barnett Hall, after Clara had excused herself to go the bathroom, Arthur had found directions scribbled on a notepad to Doug's Save and Pawn in the bottom of the gypsy's tote.

Arthur's eccentricities amused Felipe. On that eventful day he watched from the patio, smoking a cigarette, the interaction between Clara and Arthur. She gave Victor's brother a gift wrapped in tissue paper and pointed to the tie as Arthur held it up to the light. He touched her hand for a second, but her face hardened, and she left the table. She took only her wallet to pay for her order; Arthur stuck his hand inside her bag and pulled out a slip of paper and a lipstick tube.

Later the same day, Arthur showed Felipe the info on the scrap of paper and the ties. "She still despises me, but she gave me some of Victor's favorite ties. This one is a rare find, a vintage Kiton cashmere silk knit tie. Green isn't my color, but it's worth about five hundred dollars."

Arthur ate his melon and boiled egg while he rambled on about LaShaska. "You were clever to use social media to find Ossie's sister. What a mess she is. An aspiring nightclub Betty looking after all those wild-haired children in a cramped apartment." He wrinkled his nose. "A rather distasteful place to live."

LaShaska turned out to be a woman who loved taking selfies at nightclubs with everyone including her brother. She wasn't hard to track down. During their visit to her apartment a little boy in diapers had tried to cling to her leg, and she had brushed him away. LaShaska didn't like Clara, and for a little cash donation to supplement her home daycare service she was more than glad to disclose Ossie's hangouts and girlfriends' names. Arthur had sworn in his British accent that Ossie wouldn't be hurt. "We just want our painting back," he said.

Felipe drank his tepid coffee and took a bite of his eggs. He watched Arthur push his plate aside and resume reading his paper.

"Any word from your macho cousin?" Arthur pulled his bifocals down his nose and adjusted his newspaper to see Felipe. "I do hope Doug has the Hopper stashed at the pawnshop. It will make everything simpler — unless your cousin decides to shoot first and ask questions later. Again."

Felipe turned up the volume on the television. A bitter, metallic taste filled his mouth as the newscaster spoke about a shooting off Glenwood Road, one dead and one in critical condition in the hospital, as the screen showed Felipe's cousin strapped to a gurney being lifted inside an ambulance.

I changed buses again. My first bus had traveled into the city of Decatur, the opposite direction from where I needed to go, and I suspected the second bus I caught at the East Lake MARTA Transit Station had looped back around on Ponce de Leon Avenue.

My mind attempted to sort out the shooting scene. I was fairly certain when I got off at Ponce and Moreland Avenue, and caught a third bus, I was headed in the right direction to reach my motel. I wanted to get home. The low-battery warning on my cellphone made it impossible to check my location, or the local news reports.

Instinct told me Doug was dead, but for now, I couldn't confirm, or do anything. An elderly woman seated next to me fell asleep, clutching her shopping bag and purse as her head swayed back and forth in rhythm with the bus stops and starts. I noticed a gold Greek Orthodox cross necklace around her neck. I left her alone.

After we crossed Freedom Parkway, I recognized Little Five Points from a tourist brochure I'd read in the motel lobby. This section of Moreland contained funky boutiques and eateries, including a burger joint named the Vortex with an entrance depicting a molded skull. I spotted a 1950s-looking Zesto with an image of a giant chocolate-dipped cone in the window display. My stomach growled, but I didn't get off the bus until I reached Moreland Avenue and Memorial Drive. I wondered whether the convenience store at the gas station or the vending machine at my motel would have the cheapest junk food. Too tired to care, I bought a bag of chips and an iced tea at the station, munched, and trudged up the hill to the motel.

The ride back to the motel had taken over two hours. I was broke and out of ideas.

In my room I poured a double vodka and waited for the warmth to flood my body. I thought about calling Hernando, as if the situation wasn't messy enough already. I picked up my dead cell and plugged it in. After I gulped the last of the vodka straight from the bottle, I opened my suitcase, pulled out the blessing quilt, and hugged it to my chest. It wasn't logical, but it smelled like all the women in my family, my aunts and my mother. It smelled like the clan, like my childhood home. I spread the quilt out on the bed and crawled from square to square as I read the blessings out loud: "'May you have many children, experience deep joy and sorrow, and die an old wise woman after knowing many happy years of a great love.'"

I laid down my head and sobbed. A knock on the door made me sit up. My heart raced. Had Felipe found me? The Feds?

"Clara, open the door. This is Hernando. Please, I must speak with you."

I fumbled with the safety latch and unlocked the door. I pulled him inside my room and pushed him against the wall. I kissed him until I thought I would drown.

★ ★ ★ ★ ★

When I awoke, Hernando was pulling on his jeans. He smiled. "I need to go. My Alexandria is with a neighbor. Call me later."

I nodded. "What time is it?"

"Almost midnight."

I touched his arm. "How did you find me?" He understood I meant was it easy to track me.

"Felipe wants his Girl back, and revenge. However, my brother knows you do not have the painting." His eyebrows furrowed. "But you shouldn't wait too long to fly out of the country. Arthur has returned to England, and I'm afraid restraint left with him." He drummed his chest. "Now, back to me. I am a brilliant, lucky man. I called every motel, drove everywhere, and asked for you by your favorite fake name."

"Drew Lane," we said together. The alias combined the two female characters my mentor taught me to love, Nancy Drew and Lois Lane.

I scooted up in bed and tucked the sheet in my armpits leaving my bare shoulders exposed. "I bet you remembered how much Victor and I liked watching movies at the Starlight Drive In and narrowed your search to Moreland Avenue. You are stupendous."

He grinned.

"I'll never pooh-pooh pillow talk again," I said.

"I adore our pillow talk. I remember everything." He stroked my cheek. "Don't worry. We will find a way. Enough money for you to leave." He frowned and laid some cash on the nightstand. "For now. I wish it were more."

"No. Hernando."

He kissed my shoulder. "I will sleep better knowing you're all right. Please be careful. I love you." He turned to leave, and I saw a dimple flicker in his profile as I absorbed the warm jolt of hearing him say those big three words.

I wanted to respond with the promises people in love say, but instead I said, "Go. Before I drag you back down into this bed."

The next morning I stretched in bed and an instantaneous craving for salty and tangy mango salsa, my favorite, overwhelmed me. I rolled over and smelled Hernando's scent on the pillowcases. I wanted more of him.

The motel phone rang, but when I picked up no one was on the line. I counted the money Hernando left me and decided the complimentary breakfast of dry cornflakes with a tasteless bagel waiting for me downstairs could be brought back to my room for supper. The refrigerator was second rate, but the freezer might keep the milk for a few hours. For now, salsa would have to wait. I needed protein, an egg-cheese sandwich on dry raisin toast, and real coffee.

I repacked my suitcase, folding the blessing quilt, and threw the vodka bottle in the trash. I should curb my drinking…at least the drinking alone. I grabbed my toiletries and headed for the bathroom when I noticed an unstamped manila envelope on the floor near the door. I tried to steady my hands as I opened the sealed packet. I shook the contents on the bed. Two blue velvet drawstring bags wrapped in bubble wrap dropped out. A wad of cash and a diamond bracelet with a note were in the bags. The note read:

> Do not worry, Drew Lane. I found you because the owner of the motel where I am staying on Memorial Drive owns your motel too, and he owes me many favors. He searched for your made-up names for me.
>
> I know you say you don't believe in the old ways, the true sight, but I dreamed you were trapped in a dark dungeon with a beast scratching outside

the door. Your mother, a wise woman, agrees with me. A priest has blessed her wedding bracelet to ward off any bad spirits. Please wear it. Check the islands off the coast of Vrsar to find Roman. I contacted Sadye through her mother, long story, but we, your family, send you money for your journey to come. Your ancestors are watching over you, my dear niece, but beware. The men with olive skin, one truly loves you, and the other with hooded charcoal eyes plots your death. He is your Medusa. Travel with the wind to your back. May we meet again in the next life.

    With love and devotion,
    Your Great Aunt Amorosa

P.S. I have seen what you know to be true. I have cursed Victor's brother with blurry vision and a rash that turns into boils when he comes too near a child.

★ ★ ★ ★ ★

The doctor left Felipe and his cousin in the hospital room with the so-so news. "I'm sorry about your temporary paralysis, but a swollen spine is better than a fractured one," Felipe said. "With physical therapy or whatever you'll be…" Felipe took out a pack of cigarettes and replaced it in his pocket. "At least Doug's dead. Nice headshot."

Felipe's cousin remained silent. One side of his face and neck were wrapped in gauge bandages.

"How many rounds were fired?" Felipe asked.

"Too many to count."

Felipe noticed in the overhead lighting his cousin's gray hairs tucked among his dark curls. "The shot through your cheek should heal nicely, or so the doctor thinks, but it's not his face. Huh?" Felipe tapped on the bed railing.

A blond female in green scrubs brought in a tray of food and disappeared with her head down, her ponytail hiding the side of her face.

Felipe read the menu receipt and fidgeted with the paper. "How do they expect you to feed yourself this slop? I mean, your dexterity is messed up. Your arms work part-time." He hit the button for the nurse. "I'm not mad at you, but the police went back and found the Hopper after they pulled up Doug's phone messages. Dumbass Clara laid it all out for them. She left several messages asking about whether the painting had been sold yet and asking how to get ahold of Ossie for her cut."

The wounded man grunted.

Felipe tore the menu in half. "I'm going to kill the bitch."

Felipe's cousin eyed the I.V. bag. "Need more dope."

"Sure. Let me find a nurse. I'll be right back." He grabbed a cigarette from the pack before he reached the nurse's station and held it below the desk. "My cousin needs assistance in room D-12. He is in pain. While you're in there you might want to feed him. He is partially paralyzed."

"No smoking on hospital grounds." Miss Pretty with flawless ivory skin cocked her head and leaned forward. "He's on a standard morphine drip, but I could ask the doc to up the dosage." She smiled. "If…you go back and feed your cousin, I'll show you where we smoke. My break is in fifteen."

Thirty minutes later in the backseat of her Outback, Nurse Emily threw her head back screaming "Oh, God, that's it," and climaxed. She dismounted Felipe. "Thanks, baby. I gotta get back."

Felipe gripped her elbow and dangled the Subaru's key fob in the air. "Hey, don't leave me like this." He locked the doors.

Fear flashed across the nurse's girl-next-door face.

A thirty-something woman walked by in the parking lot discussing business on her cellphone and dragging a pharmaceutical briefcase on wheels behind her. She never glanced toward the nurse's Subaru and got into a white compact with business logos plastered on side windows and doors.

Felipe let go of Nurse Emily. "Just playing." He gave her the key fob, but he made her tug twice to retrieve it. "I mean fair is fair. Blue balls hurt." He resettled himself, scooting his manhood toward her.

She hesitated. "Okay, sure, handsome." She rubbed his erect penis through his briefs.

He waited until the pharmaceutical rep backed out her ad-on-wheels and drove off, and then Felipe pulled Miss Pretty's head down and she stroked him with her mouth. As he came he imagined Clara naked.

Hernando asked me to take some photos. He handed me his cellphone, and whispered he wanted to rip off my sundress ASAP. He was a welcome distraction, but I needed to stay alert. I couldn't believe I was in the same room with Felipe in Hernando's home after all that happened.

A truce of sorts had been called.

"Congratulations!" Felipe said. He kissed Alexandria's cheek and handed her a gift envelope. "The Curtis Institute of Music in Philadelphia means you're a recognized gifted student and on your way. I am so proud of you. Speech."

Friends crowded around and applauded. I took a few more photos of Alexandria's girlfriends, a trio who loved to scream and throw confetti. There were several adults in the room I hadn't met, but Savage and his wife stood next to a couple dressed in designer clothes and wearing expensive jewelry. I made him for a middle-aged banker, or CEO of an investment firm. She fit the Hollywood mold for beauty: a long-haired blond, maybe thirty, with big boobs. She wore gorgeous red Manolo Blahnik heels that showed off waxed, tan legs.

Alexandria pushed back the balloons in her way, their streamers tied to the armrest of a dining room chair. "Thank you, Uncle. I can't believe it. Only a hundred kids get in each year. I'll get to sing with the Philharmonic Orchestra and tour...maybe in Europe." She clapped her hands and jumped up and down.

Felipe moved closer to his niece. "Please continue with your speech. When you are finished, we eat cake."

The group cheered. I didn't. Ossie's peeps had followed Hernando to my motel and issued Mr. Z's orders to attend this celebration. How he knew about the party I couldn't guess. Ossie told Hernando he and his men would play the role of bodyguards for the event and protect me. My lover was ecstatic and refused to see the dangers hidden behind Mr. Z's real motivation.

I couldn't identify any of the serious-looking young men dressed in black sports outfits except Dewayne. He would make a call about every twenty minutes, and the others rotated locations while one of them took a stroll through the house. Otherwise, they stood with their backsides against the living and dining room walls, watching the merry throng.

Alexandria clasped her hands in front of the black polka-dot bow centered at the bodice of her dress and composed herself. "This is a dream come true, but I couldn't have done it without everyone in this room, Papa, and Uncle Felipe." She took a ragged breath.

Hernando stepped forward and hugged his daughter's shoulders. "And of course, a special thanks to Alexandria's mentor, Doctor Evelyn Fannin and her husband,

Doctor Michael Savage, of Emory University. They wrote the letters of recommendations for the full scholarship. We are so grateful for believing in my little girl when her talent was a fragile bud, nurturing her, and bringing her to the attention of an anonymous donor."

Everyone clapped except the six men in black stationed around the perimeter of the room. Alexandria seemed to accept the security as if she was already a celebrity.

Savage looked like he'd swallowed a toad, but Evelyn wiped away tears. She was the fortunate teacher who'd found the rare talent, the songbird with perfect pitch. The one who comes along once in a lifetime and makes it all worthwhile. Hernando asked Evelyn to speak.

Felipe yielded his spot to Evelyn and moved to the back of the room a few feet from me, a young couple between us.

Evelyn said, "Many months ago a child of ten years old surpassed her professor's knowledge and understanding of the miracle of music."

She raised her palms in the air. "There is nothing left I can teach Alexandria. I will miss witnessing her genius, but alas, as any good mentor knows we must release our students into the world. Let them go. As Kahlil Gibran describes in his famous poem in *On Children*, 'You are the bows from which your children as living arrows are sent forth.'"

She lifted her glass. "May you hit your mark, or your note —" She paused for the crowd's laughter to die down. "Be strong and true, my fearless Alexandria."

I could now clearly see Felipe in my peripheral view. As I took another photo I felt his oppressive presence fill the now-empty space on my right.

The guests exploded in their appreciation for the modest mentor and her well wishes for Alexandria.

"The security here is ridiculous. I give you my word. Eventually I will enjoy watching you die." Felipe used a casual tone and looked straight ahead, smiling and clapping with the others.

As I turned to go, he clamped his hand around my wrist. "Slowly. I will not be merciful."

Dewayne appeared out of nowhere, separating us. He hovered several feet above Felipe. He used his white voiceover pronunciation. "Sir, you are wanted by Miss Alexandria in the front to cut the cake." He waved his basketball-sized hand like a concierge. "This way, please."

Felipe grinned. "Please excuse me, Miss Blythe, we'll finish our conversation later."

I escaped outside to the front porch to get away from the noise and clear my head. I wondered if Mr. Z was close by when I noticed a gold Caddy sedan parked, blocking the entrance to the driveway. He stepped from the shadows. "Would you like a cigarette, Miss Clara?"

"I don't smoke, but you go ahead," I said.

He lit his cigarette as he walked up the steps. "You don't seem surprised."

"I sort of felt…" I blushed. "You have an energy that's hard for me to ignore."

"Yeah, I caught your vibe in the office the first time we met. Too bad you're white and on the run."

I grinned despite myself. "Not to mention Hernando."

"We'll never know what would've happened if I let myself..." He caressed the side of my face and rubbed a strand of hair between his fingertips.

I closed my eyes and breathed him in. His musty smell reminded me of cut tobacco leaves. Intoxicating.

He stepped back. "I wanted to warn you," he said. "It's more than likely it will get messy. You need to leave the party early, and go to the Atlanta airport tonight, and not come back." He handed me a plane ticket.

"But I thought —"

"Was never after you, not to harm you. Although I was pissed off about losing the painting, again, until my inside guy at headquarters took it from the property room for me." He flashed a dimple. "Nice video of you at the pawnshop."

Pain radiated down the back of my neck. "Great," I said.

"The ticket, compliments of my auntie. Her FBI contacts can't move on Felipe. The asshole is an asset, or informer."

"You mean the FBI knew all along about our heist?"

"Yes and no. It's complicated. His handler chose not to share all the information with management." He took a long drag, held in the smoke but managed to speak, though he sounded strained. "I can't stop him with a bullet, my original plan, but you can." He pulled a small plastic baggie from his pocket containing a tiny blue pill. "Fentanyl. It should take about fifteen minutes to kick in. Put it in his drink, and then make a farewell toast."

I shook my head.

He stepped on his cigarette butt. "You know he will hound you until the day he finally kills you. I can leave it for one of my guys. Dewayne has developed quite a crush on you."

"I don't want him involved."

Mr. Z held my gaze. "He is already in the know. You think this is his first date? Dewayne took out his father at twelve. The bastard never beat his mother again."

Laughter from the festivities permeated the walls creating a moment of irony for me. Afterward, the crickets filled the silence as I struggled with the dilemma.

"Look, I need to go." He slapped the clear baggie in my hand and rolled my fingers around it. "Do it, don't do it, or pass it on to Dewayne. It's up to you. Just remember Roman and Sadye are your family now. You put them in jeopardy if you let him live."

Dewayne nodded at me when I came back in the living room. His buddies came off as competent as a Presidential security detail. They still surrounded the perimeter of the dining and living rooms.

I realized Savage and his wife were gathering their things to leave. Felipe passed by me as he walked the Emory couple to the door, but I wasn't prepared to act. He put his drink on a side table as he shook Savage's hand. I fumbled in my breast shirt pocket and dropped the bag on the hardwood floor close to edge of the area rug where Felipe was standing. I couldn't get to it without him noticing. Panic spread through my body.

Dewayne swooped in and picked up the bag and dumped the pill in Felipe's glass using his backside as a cover. He bumped Felipe's shoulder in the process.

Felipe turned. "What the…"

"Sorry, Mr. Ménages. I saw Ms. Blythe's earring drop on the floor," Dewayne said, "and I didn't want you to step on it."

With my fingertips I covered the ear angled away from Felipe's view.

"Oh, my," I said.

Dewayne handed me nothing but air, but expertly, as if he'd practiced this sleight of hand a thousand times.

"Thank you, Dewayne," I said, and readjusted my diamond stud earring.

Felipe wasn't paying attention. He walked outside with Savage and his wife.

Dewayne said in a low voice, "It's been real." He handed me my purse from a hat rack close to the door. "There's a car and driver waiting out back for you."

"But the —"

"I'll stand by, make sure Felipe finishes his drink. Then a taxi ride before he passes out here. Don't want 911 guys to show up and have a chance to play the Narcan card."

"Narcan?"

"Bring his sorry ass back," Dewayne said. He brushed my elbow. "Hernando knows you're out of here, but..." He glanced down at the table. "Not about the blue pill."

Dewayne crossed his arms. "Go on. I'm shutting down this party soon."

I swallowed a thank you and threaded my way through the throng of people to the back door, and thought of how in the future Alexandria would associate this day with her uncle's death, not her triumph, and how I was responsible.

When I went out the back door of my lover's home and entered the backseat of the black Lexus accepting the eventuality of what I helped to set in motion, I became an accessory to murder. As the driver turned out of Reynoldstown and headed down I-75/85 to the airport, I felt the change…an animal instinct to survive no matter the cost. I was no longer a con artist, a thief. I had crossed a moral line within the short span of an hour, and I couldn't go back. Hernando had looked at me with such love and trust before the party. The woman he loved no longer existed.

Halfway to the airport I made the call. Hernando didn't pick up. It went to voice mail. I tried again. Hernando answered with the high of the moment still in his voice. "I'm so glad you called, I wanted to say goodbye. When Alexandria gets settled at Curtis I will visit —"

"Stop. Please listen. The drink on the side table by the hat rack, did Felipe finish it?"

"What are you talking about? He drank way too many drinks in every room."

"I'm serious. It could be a life or death situation."

"Now you're frightening me." I could hear Hernando move about the room. "The neighbors are cleaning up. I don't see a glass on that table."

"Where are Dewayne and the other security guys? Your brother?"

"I guess they're gone, but my inebriated brother is passed out on the couch."

"Call 911. Your brother has overdosed on Fentanyl. Tell the medics to bring Narcan to counteract the overdose."

"My God, Clara. Did you, or Dewayne…" The hard edge of anger filled his voice. "Repeat the names of the drugs."

"Fentanyl and Narcan." I spelled the names. I could hear Hernando's cellphone beep in the background as he took notes. "I am sorry I didn't tell you sooner."

The phone cut off. I tried to take a deep breath. I couldn't. I felt the heavy weight of guilt persist. I was culpable no matter what happened.

I went straight to the gate wearing the brunette wig displayed on my passport and checked in. Someone had thrown my suitcase in the Lexus complete with all my possessions from the motel. I didn't even care if they'd pawed through my personal things. I wasn't that Clara anymore. Inside an airport bathroom stall, I dug to the bottom of the suitcase for my blessing quilt and found some comfort in touching it.

Afterward, I sat near the laptop-recharging zone and powered up before I found the seating area next to the trashcan where most people avoided.

In an hour the attendant called the passengers with business-class tickets to board. I reread a line from my Kindle for the third time when a text popped on my screen:

we r at hospital papa UPSET! 😫 uncle drank too much ok now ☹️ stomach pumped wish we ✈️ for goodbye 💀 to mr. roman 🖤

What a dumbass I'd been. I put my phone on airplane mode. I couldn't wait to down a double vodka and tell the stewardess to keep them coming. I planned on drinking myself into oblivion all the way to Croatia.

Croatia: Six Months Later

I waddled from my hostess stool toward the register and my bartender. "Do you have enough kunas in the register?"

Niko, the young bartender with peach fuzz on his chin, gave me a thumb up. He didn't look old enough to be mixing his signature drink concoctions, but he had shown me a fake I.D. that had revealed him to be seventeen. It was for my benefit. The police didn't care. They looked the other way at clubs and restaurants because everybody has drunk beer at home from an early age.

The owner and our silent partner of sorts sat at the bar. He had hired the talented bartender, a natural at tending bar — a powerhouse of energy. Rade Visnjic's presence and his affable Niko had bridged the gap of mistrust the locals felt for foreigners and had made customers feel comfortable and welcome. The young man served an espresso, a newspaper, and one of Sadye's homemade biscuits to Rade as if this man of a certain age was the king of Croatia.

I shook my head. Life takes us strange places. The last six months my entire world had upended. After my flight landed in Croatia from America, I found Roman and Sadye off the coast of Vrsar on the island of Sveti Juraj, or Island of Saint George. They were enjoying the famous goat cheese about halfway through another food tour of the coastal islands. Rade, their new best friend, popped up everywhere we went. He bought us copious amounts of the local beers and wines. Sadye and I preferred the local wines, but Roman and Rade always drank beer, or Rakija, their high-alcohol version of *grappa*. At first I thought the man flashing the cash was playing us when he offered us the manager and chef jobs in his closed café in Vrsar.

He said, "I reopen and make money off American food. Croatians and tourists want new tastes mixed in with familiar food."

The con artists were being conned. I expected the buy-in to be substantial. However, when I confirmed my morning sickness was the natural progression of my pregnancy and my baby bump showed up one morning, Roman insisted we settle down. As it turned out our cash investment was minimal, but our elbow grease quite a bit more than expected to renovate and reopen the café.

We travelers became what we feared most, *Sintis* with bills to pay and jobs. We found Croatians liked some American food. Sadye and Roman learned to make American dishes with a hint of local cuisine. Pizza with prosciutto ham and pineapple was popular in the evenings when Sadye could get pineapple. Few patrons ate breakfast. Preferring their own crusty white bread, only a handful of locals bought biscuits on their way to work, but Sadye made biscuits for Roman and Rade every morning. Coffee and fresh bakery bread sustained most people until they took their midday snacks of meats and cheeses between nine and eleven, but then they ate their main meal of the day at lunch. Many Croatians skipped supper, or only snacked in the evenings.

I checked over the luncheon menu sample for today and gave my floor manager the heads up to print forty copies. The sign out front stated we opened at eleven in the morning, but Rade's neighbors, young and old, knocked on the door, and he welcomed them inside for a coffee and a chat, his ritual for special friends on their way to work or the market. After I officially unlocked the door, the ten tables with four chairs each would be full within minutes of patrons drinking a beer or wine and ordering Southern-style collard greens and fried fish. It would be a madhouse until midafternoon.

I rubbed my lower abdomen in slow circles to ease the cramps caused by the baby's movements. Victor — I'd already named him — liked to kick.

Roman walked by in his chef whites and bent down close to my belly. "Good morning, little one. This is your Uncle Roman." He kissed me on the cheek. "How is my Tinkerbelle?"

"I'm fine, but my stomach feels like a punching bag. The doctor told me the baby is developing right on schedule, but I swear this one is strong enough to take over the world, right now."

"You lay down." He pointed upstairs. "After the lunch crowd leaves, I'll get Goran to set up tables for dinner. You take load off."

I protested, and Roman pursed his lips. "Your feet, they're swollen over your shoes. Pitiful feet. They say help, help." My ballerina flats did seem a size too small, and my lower back hurt already.

"Okay, you win, but Goran forgets to sweep the floors."

"I'll handle. You rest. Sadye has a new idea for supper pizza recipe using thyme and dill with Prosciutto. What you think?"

I shrugged. "It might work."

After the midday break, the restaurant reopened at five and advertised mostly a thin pizza and snacks with a little extra surprise. The extra being a daily-special appetizer dish featuring either Sadye's Southern, down-home cooking, or Roman's take on a Russian recipe he disguised as Ukrainian with an American twist. Sometimes they combined the two, but they never named the entree anything but The Sundown Special, after Croatia's beautiful sunsets.

Rade's cuckoo clock in the office struck ten as I passed down the hallway and made my rounds through the kitchen.

Goran was chopping vegetables, and Sadye was taking out some fresh pies from the oven.

"Everything okay in here?" I asked. "Do you need any last-minute items?"

"No, we're good," Sadye said. She arranged the small pies on a cooling rack on the center stainless steel work counter. Roman smiled and put dough in an automatic pasta cutter, his holdout gadget from America.

I breathed in the aroma of the herbs and spices and the fresh baked goods. Sadye's pies were big sellers after she switched from hard-to-find berries to mini-pies with cheese filling. She wanted to broker a deal to mass produce them under Rade's tutelage. I was worried about the possible notoriety, but she and Roman, a formidable pair when of one mind, usually got their way on business matters.

Maybe it was the hormones, but Sadye's ways didn't bother me as much as they used to. I let her be alpha female on most issues, except when it came to the baby. She wanted me to go to a Western doctor for my checkups, but I liked the doctor Rade recommended in the state-sponsored clinic. I returned to the front and plopped down next to him at the bar.

Rade pinched my cheek. "Not too much longer, and we'll have a baby boy." He liked to remind me in his way he wanted to fulfill the role of Grand Papa to my child. He stood up from the barstool and stretched his legs. "It's time for my walk. I'll be back soon. Do you need anything from the market?"

"Nope, we're set. You stay away from all those widows on your walk. We don't need any more heart problems." Rade had a mild angina attack three months ago the day before we had reopened.

He pounded his stomach. "I'm fit as any man half my age. Sex keeps me young." He put on a light beige jacket and brown fedora hat. "I'm meeting Frank for chess today in the park, but tomorrow…" His eyes gleamed. "Who knows?"

"Exactly." A familiar male voice said from behind me. "Life is full of surprises."

I swung around on my stool.

Hernando stood in the entryway.

After an awkward introduction, Rade left us alone. Hernando still stood near the hallway. "I should've called first, but I wasn't sure I had the correct café until I saw Roman and Sadye in the kitchen."

"Oh, yes."

Holding red and white roses, he looked around the café. He was dressed in ashen-colored dress slacks and a white button-down shirt. "I have come from Felipe's funeral in Spain," he said, voice full of emotion. "He died in a bar fight in Madrid."

"I'm sorry to hear…" I couldn't finish the sentence. I was glad Felipe was dead.

He looked down and gave himself a moment to recover. "But the Ménages family is from northeastern Spain in Gerona."

"Yes, I remember you mentioned how beautiful northern Spain is. I am so sorry, but—"

The unconscious tension I had been carrying since my last threatening encounter with Felipe six months ago released from my body. I noticed my hands were shaking and clasped them on top of the bar.

He smiled as if reading my mind. "It's all right. The funeral was held in Gerona, and I wanted to see you, to give you the flowers that ask for forgiveness." He lifted the roses, and then lowered the bouquet near his side.

"For what?"

"I didn't know Felipe threatened your life again at Alexandria's party until Sadye called me. I don't understand why I needed to defend my brother and pretend he was blameless. Or why I didn't call you."

I stood up and walked around the bar counter toward him. "We both made mistakes." His eyes focused on my belly.

I felt the baby kick. "I'm not the same person you knew in so many ways. We have a lot to talk about, I'm glad you're here."

"The child?" He brought his hands to his mouth as in supplication.

"Is ours."

He smiled and closed his eyes for a second. "I must touch you. Please." He held his arms out and waited. He looked at me as if I was the most beautiful woman in the world. I went to him. He embraced me, and I felt a barrier crumble inside me. Tears rolled down my cheeks. He was the father of my baby. I missed him. I loved him.

Hernando spoke as he cupped a gentle hand behind my head, "It will be all right. No matter what happens, or what you decide, I love you."

"We will work this out."

* * * * *
THE END

ABOUT THE AUTHOR

Lynn Hesse was the 2015 First Place Winner, Oak Tree Press, Cop Tales, for her mystery, *Well of Rage*. Her novel *Another Kind of Hero* was a finalist for the 2018 Silver Falchion Award and won the International Readers' Favorite Chill Award in 2021. Her short story "Jewel's Hell" was published September 2019 in *Me Too Short Stories: An Anthology* by Level Best Books and edited by Elizabeth Zelvin. Her short story "Bitter Love" was accepted for publication in *Crimeucopia's* October 2021 issue for Murderous Ink Press, United Kingdom.

Her short story about a domestic homicide, "Murder: Food For Thought", published in the anthology *Double Lives, Reinvention & Those We Leave Behind, 2009* by Wising Up Press, was adapted in the play, *We Hunt Our Young*, produced at Emory University Field Showcase and Core Studio Luncheon Time Series, 2011. Excerpts from the play "Unacceptable Truths" about domestic abuse were performed on the Atlanta BeltLine in 2013.